WILLIAM ESMONT

THE PATRIOT PARADOX

A Kurt Vetter and Amanda Carter Thriller

Edition 2.0, May 2011

Copyright © 2010 by William Esmont
ISBN: 978-1505666878

www.williamesmont.com

DISCLAIMER
This is a work of fiction. All the characters and events portrayed in this book are fictional, and any resemblance to real people or incidents is purely coincidental.

DEDICATION

For Robin, who continues to support my quest to become a fulltime author. And for my parents, who taught me the value of a good story.

ACKNOWLEDGMENTS

I'd also like to give special thanks to Gretchen Cooke, Becky Smith, and Don Query for taking the time to critique this novel as it evolved. This wouldn't be possible without your input. Finally, I'd like to thank Chris Muller, who took a mediocre cover and made it shine. Thank you!

One

MIKE VETTER HATED THIS KIND of weather. Rain. Endless, miserable rain. Relentless torrents of misery pissed from swollen black clouds above the treetops. Aside from the occasional flash of chalky white lightning and the pathetic illumination from his headlights, he could see nothing of the road ahead.

This is what it feels like to drown.

He tightened his grip on the steering wheel and peered through the furious *slip-slap* of his wipers. He blinked and rubbed his eyes. Red lights twinkled through the shifting curtains of rain.

"Shit!" Mike jumped on the clutch and brake simultaneously with all of his might. His Audi hydroplaned for an interminable moment, the rear end threatening to break loose, and then juddered hard as the tires bit pavement and the antilock brakes kicked in. A moment later, he jolted to a stop inches behind an old Ford Explorer.

He tensed, bracing for impact from the rear. When it didn't come, Mike opened his eyes in time to see a semi-trailer roar by on his left, missing his side mirror by inches. He checked his rear-view mirror and breathed a sigh of relief. It was clear.

The traffic lurched to life again, and Mike pushed the Audi back up to speed. Through a brief gap in the rain, he saw what he had been looking for, an office park at the bottom of the next exit ramp.

Almost missing his turn, he cut across two lanes of traffic, triggering a barrage of angry horn blasting. A minute later, he pulled to a stop a few yards short of a lone FedEx drop box and knocked his car into neutral.

He looked around to make sure he was alone, then opened his glove box and dug out a small flash memory card. He placed it in the FedEx envelope in his lap and sealed the envelope tight, going over it twice to make sure it was secure. As an afterthought, he took his gun from the front seat and stuffed it into the glove box.

He fished a billing label from his pocket and jotted down a long string of digits. The account number was stolen, but the seller from Craigslist had guaranteed it would be good for at least a week. That was six days more than he needed. He paused for a moment, tapping his pen against the steering wheel and chewing his lip as he considered whether he had made the right decision.

"Screw it." He scribbled a name and address on the label and stuffed it into the pouch on the front of the envelope. He inched the car forward until he reached the drop box.

The rain swept in, drenching him to the skin as his window descended. He stretched out, stuffed the envelope into the drop box slot, and jabbed the window button, restoring the barrier between him and the storm.

Mike got back onto the interstate. *This is it.* Technically, he had committed high treason. Was it really treason, though, if he was doing the right thing? If he was the only one willing to stop a lunatic? A wave of doubt washed over him. *Maybe we were right. Maybe.* He pushed the thoughts aside. It didn't matter anymore.

He saw a hole in the traffic and mashed down on the accelerator. He drove on autopilot for the next twenty minutes, not really paying attention to where he was going, just moving.

The rain tapered off as he approached the Haymarket exit. His car chimed, jolting him back to the moment. "What the hell?" He checked the instrument cluster and saw that the fuel light was on. Scanning the road ahead, he saw a well-lit, but empty BP station at the bottom of the exit. He cut the wheel hard and darted down the ramp and into the station, pulling around to the pumps farthest from the highway.

Mike killed the engine, got out of the car, and reached for the premium nozzle. On the other side of the island, a metallic-blue Cadillac sedan rolled to a stop, wet tires chirping on the dry cement pad. Startled, Mike turned at the noise. Riding low to the ground, the Caddy looked fast even standing still. On any other day, he would have been impressed. Turning back to his pump, he swiped his credit card and stabbed the nozzle into his tank. From the other car, he heard the hum of an electric window rolling down. He glanced over, curious.

"Mike Vetter." It was more of a statement than a question. The man who had spoken from the front passenger seat was about Mike's age, clean-cut and nondescript with shaggy brown hair and a medium build. *Agency.*

A wave of crippling nausea washed through him as he realized they had caught up with him. He was going to die right here, right now. Years of training kicked in, sending him scurrying away from the Cadillac, seeking cover behind a thick concrete pillar that stretched from the ground to the roof far above. *My gun*, he thought in a panic, *it's in the car!*

Peeking around the pillar, he saw the man in the Cadillac signal to his driver. Mike made a break for his Audi. With a guttural roar, the Cadillac jumped forward and cut hard to the right, blocking his exit.

At that moment, Mike reached his door and hauled on the handle. Some sense of morbid curiosity, however, made him look up at the Cadillac. Mike recognized the look, the dead eyes, the feigned indifference at the razor-thin line between life and death. It was impossible to miss, for it was the same look he himself had cultivated a lifetime ago as a new CIA recruit at Langley.

He froze. That was all the time the man in the Cadillac needed. As Mike stared, the man drew a compact matte-black pistol from his jacket, leveled it at Mike's face, and pulled the trigger.

Mike's last thoughts, of his wife and children, flew through the back of his skull at four hundred and fifty feet per second.

Two

"**U**NA MÁS, POR FAVOR," KURT mumbled from the end of the bar as he raised his glass toward the pretty bartender. She nodded. No more than nineteen, her dark eyes lingered on him just a little too long, probably curious as to what he was doing in this corner of Peru.

She topped off his glass, giving it a slight twist at the end to bust the foam, and slid it across the scarred bar to his waiting hand. "*Veinte soles, señor,*" she said, with a demure smile.

He fished a tattered wad of bills from an inner pocket of his leather jacket, ruffled through them, squinting in the dingy light of the bar, and handed over a hundred Sole note. "*Muchas gracias.*"

Her eyes lit up at the sight of the cash, and she straightened and threw her shoulders back, giving him a spectacular view of her cleavage. Her flirting wasn't lost on Kurt, but instead of acknowledging it, he took his beer, turned, and ambled out the front door.

She has potential, he noted, *and she's definitely interested.*

"*Señor!*" Kurt turned and found the bartender at his side, holding a crumpled fistful of bills, his change.

He waved her off with a smile. "No. *Gracias.* For you. *Muchas gracias.*"

He didn't have to tell her twice. With a sly grin, the girl tucked the money into her blouse. "*Gracias señor. I very much thank—*" He dismissed her with a friendly wave, handed her his half-empty glass, and continued on his way.

He was tired. Tired of the road, tired of drinking his days away alone and waking up with a different woman every week. It was a fatigue he never could have anticipated, and he couldn't figure out how to take the next step, to move beyond it. This trip was supposed to be his salvation, a chance to reconnect with the world and rediscover who he was. Instead, it had turned into a slow grind that was killing him.

Shielding his eyes against the early afternoon sun, Kurt paused outside the door and scanned the plaza spread before him. Blue tarps dominated the vista. Stretched across makeshift stalls, they served as storefronts for the hundreds of vendors hawking their wares to the tourists who flowed through the city on the way to and from the Inca trail. The tarp closest to him chuffed as a gust of wind caught it from below, reminding him of the sound of sails snapping tight at the Chesapeake Harbour Marina.

No. He shook his head. *I'm sick of this goddamned place.* He turned to the right and picked his way down the fractured sidewalk toward a side street that led to a park that didn't allow street vendors. Kurt was relieved to discover that the park was mostly deserted. Aside from a young mother and her three children, he was alone.

He chose a bench on the far side, more for the view of the mountains towering over the city than for its comfort, and took a seat. The three children scurried around the plaza chasing pigeons and screaming in delight every time they got close. Their mother appeared content to let her children burn off their energy, as she split her time between a magazine and watching them play.

Despite the blazing sun high overhead, the air still held a slight chill. Kurt shrugged back into his jacket, leaving it unzipped in a fruitless attempt to achieve a comfortable temperature. As he fiddled with his zipper, his wrist bumped against the mobile phone stashed in his breast pocket. He took it out. It had been three full weeks, no, four, since he had last spoken with anyone back home.

He flipped the phone open with his thumb and pressed the power button. It took only a moment for the phone to come to life and snatch a signal from the thin mountain air. Once it did, he saw that he had a voicemail. He accessed his voicemail and put the phone to his ear.

There was the usual burst of machine-gun Spanish as the automated recording told him how to place a call on his home network. He already knew the routine.

"You have two new messages; press one to listen to your new messages," said the soothing computer voice on the other end.

He pressed one before the voice could list the other options.

After the date and time information, he heard,

"Kurt. Hey. It's me. Listen. I've got to talk to you." There was a long silence. "It's really important. Call me as soon as you get this." Kurt made a mental note to call his brother as he deleted the message.

The next was from his mother. "Kurt. There's been an accident. Mike—he's dead. Please, please come home." Her voice dissolved into sobs, and a moment later, his father came on. "Kurt, it just happened. We don't know the details yet." His father's voice choked up for a moment, and then continued, "Call me when you get this."

Kurt closed his eyes and bit back a scream. He didn't delete this message. He closed the phone and, staring at the mountains high above without seeing them, he slumped on the bench. His stomach roiled, and he felt as if he were about to vomit. With a concentrated effort, he managed to swallow back the bile that had crept up his throat, associating the sour taste with the direction his life had taken.

His trip was over; that much was clear. It was time to leave.

Three

JACK CARSON HOISTED HIMSELF FROM his chair and went to the tinted window overlooking the lush green lawns surrounding the CIA campus. A steady rain fell, but nothing like the night before. He returned to his desk, settling into the plush, black leather executive chair that was his home away from home.

At sixty-one years old, Jack was a big fish in the small pond of the National Clandestine Service, the arm of the Central Intelligence Agency responsible for in-field intelligence gathering. The spies. He had entered the agency thirty-five years earlier, straight out of Harvard Law, after deciding a career wearing a suit for the FBI wasn't for him. A veteran of the Cold War, he had completed tours of duty in several Eastern Bloc and Southeast Asian countries before finally succumbing to the lure of a stable desk job. Despite the comfortable life within the CIA management structure, a fire still burned deep within, an all-consuming desire to finish the war his government had all but forgotten.

Standing a hair over six foot three, with a full head of steel-gray hair and a razor-sharp intellect, Jack cut an imposing figure within the halls of the agency. He was comfortable with his power and had no compunction about wielding his considerable influence to further his goals.

With a deep sigh, Jack picked up his phone and punched in a four-digit number. "My office. Bring Mason."

A minute later, there was a knock on his door. "Come in," he bellowed.

The door opened without a sound, and a man and a woman entered, the woman pushing the door shut behind her. Only thirty-one-years-old, Helen Bartholomew was an accomplished field agent with extensive experience hunting terrorists in the former Russian republics. She was also a savant at intelligence synthesis, able to see through the torrent of data that inundated the agency and pick and choose the pieces she needed. That was the reason Jack had pulled her into his division in the first place. On the pretty side of beautiful, she was the quintessential spy, able to blend into almost any crowd and learn any language.

The man beside her was another story altogether. Mason Perot was short and swarthy and always had an easy grin on his face. Ruthless, yet dependable, he had served with Helen on several missions and he knew how to make things happen.

Since the pair had begun working for him, Jack had suspected some sort of romantic entanglement, but he had never been able to put his finger on it. Regardless, they worked well together, and that was the only thing that mattered.

He reached under his desk and pressed a discreet button connected to a white noise generator. Although the office was soundproofed and swept for electronic listening devices daily, he felt there was no such thing as too much privacy. "Have a seat," he said, waving at the chairs opposite his desk.

Helen sat and crossed her legs. Mason's girth made it a tight fit in his chair, and he grumbled as he squeezed himself in.

"I just got off the phone with our friends," Jack said. "Everything is in place."

Helen and Mason both nodded, waiting for the other shoe to drop. They knew Jack wouldn't have called them in for a routine status update. They were right.

Jack adjusted his tie and narrowed his eyes. "What I need to know from the two of you is why in the hell I have complete operational control on the other side of the planet, yet one of my own people can walk out of the front of this agency with our entire plan in his back pocket? What the fuck is up with that?"

Helen and Mason shared a quick glance. Helen cleared her throat. "Jack," she said in a deferential tone, "you know how it went down. After we took Vetter out, we had less than two minutes before the local police arrived. We searched him. He was clean."

"She's right," Mason added. He had been the one to search Mike Vetter's body and vehicle after the shooting.

Jack clucked his tongue in frustration. "It doesn't make any sense. He carried classified information out of *my* office!"

Helen held up one hand. "Hold on, Jack. There was something." She fished in her pocket and pulled out a long string of white paper with a tab on one end and a hint of blue lettering along its length.

"What's that?" Jack asked, anger morphing into curiosity.

"It's a zipper from a FedEx envelope. It was on his front seat."

"Now we're getting somewhere." He let a half-smile slip onto his face. "Was there any sign of the envelope?"

Helen shook her head. "No." His smile vanished.

"There are sixty-one FedEx drop off points between here and where we took him down," Mason volunteered, looking up from his tablet.

Jack leaned back in his chair, put his elbows on the armrests and steepled his fingers. "Interesting." Jack stood and went back to the window. He stared out for a moment, considering the possibilities, then turned back. "Put a trace on his immediate family and associates. We need to know if anyone receives a package from him in the next day or two."

Helen smiled. "Already done. We've got his family as well as his civilian acquaintances covered."

"Can we trace the packages shipped from those locations?"

"Not without a warrant."

Jack raised an eyebrow.

"There's no visibility until they reach the pickup center. We were too late."

"Okay. What about the other carriers? UPS and DHL?"

"Covered."

"Good." Jack took a seat on the edge of his desk. "Consider this your top priority," he said, alternating his gaze between the two agents. "Until we understand where the information went, our entire plan is in jeopardy."

Helen asked, "Have you heard from Fish?"

Fisher "Fish" Coldwell was the third person in Jack's leadership triumvirate, the yin to Jack's yang and a royal pain in Mike Vetter's ass. Where Mike had ethics, Fish had none.

"No," Jack lied. "Not a word."

"I thought you said you just spoke with —"

Jack cut her off. "No. That was another asset in the field. None of your concern."

She frowned, obviously frustrated at his answer.

"Is that it?" Mason asked.

"Yes. We'll talk later."

Four

KURT PULLED HIS JACKET AND helmet on, and in a well-practiced motion, slung his leg over the saddle, taking care not to catch it on the bulky silver panniers protruding from the rear of the machine. He detached the key from the lanyard around his neck, jabbed it into the ignition, and fired up the bike with his right thumb. It came to life with the same buzz and clatter he had grown to love over the past months.

He looked both ways, goosed the throttle, and darted into traffic. He had seen a sign for the airport on the way into town, so he backtracked until he found it again. *Only four kilometers. Not bad.*

It took only a few minutes to reach the airport, but the trip was the typical Peruvian obstacle course of deathtrap taxis hurtling over rutted roads. He wouldn't miss that aspect of South America. Not one bit.

He pulled into the lot in front of the airport and glanced around. The sun was dipping low behind the western mountains, and long shadows reached across the asphalt. For a brief moment, he reflected on the cocoon in which he had existed for the past months. He had managed to leave the outside world behind, existing solely for the moment, whether it was climbing a mountain pass or getting to the next town without hitting a cow.

Mike is dead. He shook his head, still not sure what to make of the news. He and Mike had grown up together. His brother, four years older, had been there for him at every turn. Hell, his first girlfriend was the little sister of one of his brother's friends.

A tear came to his eye, snaking down his dusty cheek and splashing on his jacket collar. He pulled off his helmet then removed his gloves, placing them inside the helmet.

He went to the rear of the bike and unfastened his saddlebags, setting them on the ground beside the bike. He took a quick inventory of his belongings. His bike looked naked now, unloved and forlorn. It had the usual nicks and dings that were part of any long voyage, but aside from the gadgets bolted directly to the bike, it could have been anyone's machine. He turned, picked up his gear, and headed for the terminal.

He stopped at the door and scanned the room. There was only one thing left to do. No, there was something else. He surveyed the late afternoon crowd, looking from face to face, making quick mental calculations about who was about to have a lucky day. He settled on a man about his size lounging beside a newspaper stand and smoking a hand-rolled cigarette. He looked American, or maybe European, and appeared to be in his early twenties.

Kurt walked over to him. *"Hola."*

16

The man sized him up and nodded in response.

"Look," Kurt continued, "I have to leave the country. Out in the parking lot there's a BMW motorcycle. It's yellow."

The man eyed him with suspicion, still not speaking.

"Take good care of her." Kurt tossed the keys to the guy, who snatched them from the air.

"Are you kidding, mate?" *New Zealand.*

"No. It's legit. Something came up. I have to leave."

"I don't understand—" the man started, flustered.

"Oh yeah, you'll need this." Kurt fished around in the inside pocket of his jacket and extracted the title to the motorcycle. He flipped it over on the newsstand counter and grabbed a pen from the counter. Yanking the cap off with his teeth, he signed the document with a quick flourish, leaving the buyer's name blank. It would be up to the Kiwi to fill it in. Kurt put the cap back on the pen and pushed the paper across the counter.

The man stared, mouth agape. A smile blossomed on his face as he realized Kurt's offer was legitimate.

"Enjoy her. She's been good to me," Kurt said.

"Thanks, man!"

A young woman with a backpack strolled up carrying two liter-sized bottles of water.

"What's going on, Ben?" she asked. Kurt liked her accent. It sounded like she said 'Bin.'

"This bloke just gave me his bike!" the Kiwi said with a stupid grin.

"You're kidding." She turned to Kurt with a suspicious look.

He smiled. "Yep."

Ben couldn't stop grinning. "It is. He gave me the title and everything!"

"Can we give you anything?" she asked incredulously. "I mean—"

Kurt waved her off. "Don't worry about it." He turned and started towards the Delta ticket counter, leaving the Kiwis to enjoy their newfound vehicle.

"*Buenas tardes*," he said to the ticket agent.

"Good afternoon, sir," she replied in mellifluous English. "How can I help you today?"

"I need a one way ticket to Washington, DC." He slid his passport and American Express gold card across the counter. "As soon as possible." She took the card and held his stare for a long, uncomfortable moment before turning to her computer.

Five minutes later, he strolled through the security stalls. His panniers were traveling as luggage; all he carried was the small backpack he normally kept attached to his gas tank. His flight left in three hours, going first through Miami, and from there, to Dulles International, outside of Washington.

Looking around the boarding lounge, Kurt scoped out a comfortable-looking seat near his gate.

Home.

Five

KURT AWOKE AS THE PACKED Boeing 757 banked hard to the right. For a moment, he wasn't sure where he was. Then it all came back in a rush. *An airplane. Going home.*

He stretched, contorting his lanky frame in a futile effort to get his blood flowing. Opening the shade on his right, he pressed his face against the scuffed Lexan and peered out. Thick, sodden clouds enveloped the jet. Fat water rivulets streaked the window, crawling across the glass in convoluted streams. He snapped the window shade shut.

The cabin bell chimed, and a flight attendant came on the intercom, informing the passengers that they were beginning their final approach. Seatbelts secure. Tray tables upright. All of that.

Kurt had been asleep since shortly after lifting off from Miami, the stress of Mike's death serving as a potent sedative. He didn't feel refreshed, though. If anything, he felt a numbing sense of dread as his past and his future raced toward each other on a collision course.

Thirty minutes later, he was on the ground, elbowing his way through the crowds to reach the baggage carousel. Despite his best efforts, he couldn't help but be reminded of the last time he had been here, at this same carousel, meeting his wife and daughter. Amelia and Heidi. Kurt squeezed his hands tight, nails digging into his palms, cutting bloody half-moons. It helped.

Like Mike, they were gone, cut down by a speeding ambulance eleven months earlier. He squeezed harder. He felt himself slipping, starting to tumble into the well of despair he had so carefully avoided for the past four months. He gave himself a hard mental slap, an openhanded blow to the mind, and the memories went scurrying back into the dark corners of his conscience where they belonged. He wasn't ready to think about them. *Not yet.*

He had spoken with his mother during his Miami layover, calling to inform her of his travel plans. Why he hadn't called her from Peru, he wasn't sure. It didn't matter now. He was almost home.

The doors leading to the exterior of the airport whooshed open as he approached, his tank bag slung over his shoulder, and a pannier in each hand. The humidity assaulted him like an unwanted lover, pasting a thick sheen of sweat on every inch of exposed skin. He stopped and shed his dirt- and oil-encrusted leather jacket and stuffed it into one of his panniers. Picking up his luggage again, he made his way towards the taxi line. There were only two people in front of him, and at least ten taxis waiting for fares.

A late model yellow Crown Vic pulled up, and a slender Ethiopian man jumped from the driver's seat to help him load his gear. Kurt waved him off. "Thanks, I've got it."

"Are you sure?" the cabbie asked in a singsong voice.

"Uh huh." He took a step toward the trunk. The driver was persistent, holding the trunk open as Kurt dumped in his panniers.

"Where to?" the driver asked, as he slid behind the wheel.

"Forty-five Quail Court. Fairfax."

Kurt put his head back and closed his eyes, hoping the cabbie wasn't the talkative type. The cab lurched out of the pickup lane with a squeal and merged into the maelstrom of northern Virginia traffic.

The eyes-closed trick must have worked because the cabbie didn't say a word. The next thing Kurt knew, they were parked in front of his house, idling. "Keep the change," he muttered, slipping the man two twenties to cover the thirty-dollar fare.

"Of course. Have a good day, sir."

Standing three stories tall, the old brick building stared back at him with empty eyes. It had been four months since he had last set foot in the place, four months during which he had made every effort possible to forget about it and everything it represented. With a sigh, Kurt grabbed his bags and lumbered up the short sidewalk to the front door. There was a moldering pile of Washington Posts on the right side of the porch. The freshest paper bore a date a month after his exodus.

He held up his key and stared at it, watching the sunlight bounce off the small brass talisman of his former existence. It was the same key he had used at least twice a day for the three years he, Amelia, and Heidi had lived here, the same key that had been stashed out of sight in the bottom of his tank bag as he fled south.

The key sank into the lock as if no time had passed. Kurt took a deep breath and steeled himself for what was next.

After Amelia and Heidi had died, the promise of the trip was his only lifeline, the only thing that kept him moving forward. In the deep of the night, when loneliness clawed at his heart, the trip was the only thing that prevented him from eating a bullet and joining his wife and daughter in oblivion.

In a practiced motion, Kurt twisted the key and put his shoulder to the door. It swung open easily, revealing the sunny entryway of a thousand days of happiness and one terrible day of sorrow. He stepped through and inhaled. The house smelled much as he had left it, maybe a little mustier. A jumbled pile of old mail sat on a table beside the door—magazines for Amelia, business correspondence for him. In addition, peeking out from the bottom was what appeared to be an unopened birthday card for Heidi.

Kurt dropped his bag, threw his keys on the table, then kicked the door closed with his heel. He cocked his head and listened. Silence. No, not quite. The air conditioner hummed from somewhere on the other side of the house.

He made his way into the living room, where he sank into the leather couch in the darkest corner. He didn't bother with the lights; there was still plenty coming in through the glass doors on the opposite side of the room.

He put his feet up on the coffee table and pulled out his mobile phone. He had purposefully not called his mother upon arrival. He knew she would only make things more complicated by demanding to see him right away. He didn't need that. This homecoming had to happen on his terms, or it couldn't happen at all.

He thumbed the phone on and watched it gather a signal. As soon as it finished synchronizing with the network, he dialed his parents.

His mother picked up on the second ring. "Kurt?"

"Hi, Mom."

"Are you home? I tracked your flight and saw that it landed over an hour ago. Where are you?"

"Yes. I'm at home." Sweat poured from his brow despite the air conditioning.

His mother let out a long sigh. "How are you?"

He glanced around the room. "I'm okay."

"Are you sure, honey?"

Kurt rubbed his right eye, halting a stray tear in its tracks. "I'm fine. I need to do this."

"Kurt, your father wants a word."

He heard it in her voice. Things were not good between Kurt and his father. They never had been. His mom had served as the buffer between him and the old man as his life had fallen apart. She had been the only person to encourage him to take his trip, to leave everything behind, while his father had tried to act as if nothing had happened.

Kurt knew he couldn't avoid his father forever. "Okay. Put him on."

"Just a second." He heard a soft clunk and pictured her placing the phone on the table, the one beside the green sitting room armchair; the sound was followed by the click of her heels as she left the room. She would never stoop so low as to call through the house.

"Son?"

"Yeah. Hey, Dad."

"Thanks for coming…" There was a long pause. His dad coughed, cleared his throat, and continued. "Since your brother died…"

This is ridiculous, Kurt thought. He had to end this, to put his father out of his misery. "I know, Dad. I'll see you tomorrow morning at the funeral. We can talk then." He had intended to talk to his dad, to clear the air. As the last surviving Vetter son, an enormous responsibility was now on his shoulders; it was a responsibility Kurt wasn't quite sure he wanted.

His father seemed surprised by the rebuke. "Right. Tomorrow. Do you want to speak to your mother again?"

"No. This is enough for tonight."

"Okay. And Kurt?"

"Yeah?"

"I love you. Always remember that. I always have." For the first time in as long as Kurt could remember, his father sounded genuine.

"I know, Dad. I know," he responded.

The line went dead. He envisioned his father on the other end. He understood his pain. "Your children weren't supposed to die before you," and all of that bullshit his shrink had said after the accident. He knew more about loss than any one man should ever have to know.

Kurt thumbed off the phone and shoved it back in

his pocket. He shifted his feet to the couch and stretched his body the full length, the rich leather crunching and crinkling as he made himself comfortable.

It was eight o'clock. Only another hour or so of daylight remained. Already, shadows were slinking across the room, disguising the familiar shapes of his old life in dusky cloaks of black and gray. What he didn't know, and couldn't possibly fathom, was what was waiting for him on the other side of this experience. The one thing he knew for sure was that there would be a lot more pain before things got better.

He rolled onto his side and closed his eyes, finally succumbing to the cozy embrace of the couch and the familiar surroundings.

Six

KURT SAT UP AND RUBBED the sleep from his eyes. His face was greasy, and his hair was a tangled nest of road grime, salt, sweat, and maybe even a few bugs. He needed a shower, and he needed it now.

Pushing himself from the couch, finding his way by memory alone, he stumbled up the dark stairs to the master bedroom. He stopped at the doorway and leaned against the jamb for a second, taking it in. Light from a nearby street lamp cast a soft glow through the room. Someone had made the bed and cleaned up, probably his mother, maybe Mike. Whoever it was, they had done a good job. The room had never looked this clean when he and Amelia had lived here.

The bathroom was on the far side of the room. Kurt made his way across, ignoring the family portrait on the nightstand, focusing on the shower. His palm found the switch, and he squinted as the lights flickered on. His clothes went into the hamper beside the door. He held his fingers under the shower faucet and dialed the hot water almost to scalding.

He stepped into the shower and closed his eyes. Almost losing his balance, he reached for the walls to steady himself. For a terrifying moment, he thought he was going to collapse. Counting backward from ten, he forced himself to relax, just as his shrink had taught him. By the time he reached two, the world had stopped gyrating. The images of his former life dissolved into the clouds of steam billowing around him. With renewed vigor, he raced through the rest of his shower, scrubbing away the last remnants of his trip.

Five minutes later, his beard was trimmed to a more respectable length, and his unruly sideburns were gone. He promised himself he would pay a visit to the barber as soon as he dealt with Mike's funeral. For now though, his long hair would have to suffice. He pulled it back in a ponytail, holding it in place with a stray rubber band from the medicine cabinet. Good enough.

Turning, he headed into the bedroom to find some clean clothes. The room was enormous, with two walk-in closets and a king-sized bed. The closet on the left, the one with the door cracked open, was his. He was tempted to peek inside Amelia's closet, to see if her scent lingered, and found himself taking an involuntary step in that direction. He stopped. No.

He went to his closet instead, grabbing a pair of boxer briefs from a drawer on the left. As he pulled them on, he realized how much weight he had lost. The briefs hung loose on his hips, threatening to slide down his legs. From a shelf halfway up, Kurt pulled out a pair of olive green cargo shorts. Next were a navy blue web belt and a t-shirt.

Exiting the closet, he padded out of the bedroom and down the stairs, passing by Heidi's door without a glance. In the foyer, he cracked open one of his aluminum panniers and pulled out his favorite pair of sandals. Made from recycled automobile tires, they were the most comfortable shoes he owned.

"Hello, old friends," he whispered as he slipped them on.

He turned and made his way into the kitchen. *Coffee*. Grabbing his French press, he loaded it with sugar and fresh grounds, then filled the kettle and set it to boil.

The water finished boiling, but as he was about to pour it into the press, there was a sharp knock at the front door. He glanced at the clock over the microwave and cursed. *Who's knocking on my door at this hour?*

He poured the water in, gave the coffee a quick stir, set the lid on the press, and then hurried down the hall. Through the frosted window to the right of the door, Kurt made out the distorted image of a man. He opened the door to a FedEx delivery man.

"Kurt Vetter?"

"Yeah?"

"Sign here," the driver said, handing him a small electronic device and a plastic stylus.

Kurt scribbled his name in the small window at the top and handed it back.

"Thanks." The man gave him an envelope, then turned and jogged back to his truck. Kurt inspected the label on the package. The only indication of the sender's identity was a long string of digits.

He found his coffee was ready and filled his

favorite mug to the rim. Armed for the morning, he took the coffee and the letter and ambled into the dining nook, located by a large bay window with a view of the back yard.

His curiosity got the best of him; he set the coffee aside and pulled the tab on the envelope. He looked inside and didn't see anything. He turned the envelope upside down and knocked it against the table. A small flash memory card clattered out onto the table.

"Huh?" He picked up the card and inspected it. It was a Secure Digital card, the same model he had in his digital camera. His curiosity was piqued. He looked over his shoulder, searching for the laptop they kept in the kitchen. It had a flash reader.

He spied the machine buried under a pile of magazines on the counter. The battery was probably dead, but it was worth a try. The other alternative was to go up to his study and use his office computer.

Two minutes later, the computer was booted and ready. Kurt slid the memory card into a slot on the right side and waited for it to be recognized. When it was ready, the computer created a new folder on his desktop with lettering underneath indicating two items. Kurt double-clicked on the folder.

It popped open in a new window, and he saw that it contained one file, along with another directory. The second directory contained 1,342 items.

Kurt double clicked on the file, titled Listen-to-me-First.mp3, and took a sip of coffee as his audio player started up. "Kurt. It's Mike. If you're listening to this, then things have gone terribly wrong." His brother's voice was low and calm, the way Kurt remembered it.

Kurt pressed *Pause* and sat back, stunned. He

checked the time stamp on the file. Three days ago. The same day Mike had died.

He pressed *Play.* "I've gotten involved in something...something that I should have never touched. The people I work for, they've taken an idea that should have remained buried in a vault, and they're trying to make it real." There was a long pause, and Mike's voice resumed, this time a little less steady. "Tell Amy that I'm sorry and that I love her. Tell her I was a good man—that I tried to do the right thing. Tell mom and dad that I love them, too. And Kurt—I'm sorry to drag you into my problems when you've been to hell and back. I really need you, one last time. You need to get this information to Amanda Carter in London. She'll know what to do with it."

Time slowed to a crawl as he stared at the computer screen. Then, without warning, it sped back up and crashed over him like a rogue wave. He let out an anguished moan and slammed his fist down on the kitchen table so hard the computer jumped in place.

This is Mike's last message, he realized, *his last will and testament.*

He pushed back from the computer, unsure what to make of the whole thing. *Who is Amanda Carter? What's in the other folder? Moreover, why did Mike send it to him rather than going straight to her?*

As he thought about the recording, turning it over repeatedly in his mind, he was hit by a sinister realization. *They'll come for me next.*

Kurt leapt up and dashed over to the bay window. He stood to one side and peered out, trying to appear as casual as possible. He didn't see anything. With a quick yank, he closed the blinds. He repeated this process throughout the house, everywhere except Heidi's room. He still couldn't go in there.

Satisfied no one could see in, he returned to the computer. He replayed Mike's message, listening for anything he had missed. There was nothing.

He moved on, opening the other folder. A new window opened, displaying an enormous alphabetical list of files. They appeared to be of many different types, Microsoft Word documents, MPEG video files, and even some more mp3 files. He clicked on one of the video files at random.

It took a few seconds to load. The video was grainy and showed what appeared to be a campsite somewhere in the mountains. The camera panned and settled on the face of a young man with a long, scraggly beard, not unlike the one Kurt had just shaved off. The man spoke in a language Kurt didn't understand. He watched the video for a few more seconds, skipping ahead several times, but it didn't make any more sense, so he closed it.

He picked a Microsoft Word file at random. The file popped open, and he began to skim through it. It contained a long list of financial transactions between offshore accounts. He paged through the document to the end. That was it. He was getting frustrated, but an idea was forming. He selected search from the menu and entered his brother's name. *Nothing.* He scratched his head.

He decided to push the search a little farther. He minimized the document, returned to the main window, typed Mike's name into the search box, and hit *Enter.* A list of twenty-six files opened. Kurt sucked in his breath and chose the first one.

He blinked, unable to believe what he was seeing. It was Mike's CIA personnel file. He yanked his hands from the keyboard as if he had received an electric shock. The classification level on this information was so high that even Mike wouldn't have been able to view it. *Probably not even the President,* Kurt thought, *without congressional authorization.* Yet, there it was. Kurt drummed his fingers on the table, considering what to do next.

"What the hell did you get yourself into?" he whispered.

Kurt spent the next several minutes scanning his brother's records, absorbing all of the gory details concerning the secret life his brother had led for the past ten years. The last entry in the record, however, was the most intriguing, and at the same time, the least informative. It noted a transfer to a new program, yet the program was unnamed.

It listed his supervisor as a man named Jack Carson. Kurt knew the name. From where, he wasn't sure, but he had heard it on more than one occasion. He filed the information away and moved on to the next document.

He continued until he had plowed through all of the documents that contained his brother's name. As he finished the last document, he sat back in his chair and let out a deep breath. At first glance, it appeared Mike had been intimately involved in some type of money-laundering effort between the CIA and a separatist organization in Chechnya, the breakaway Russian republic. The details were murky, but the amount of money involved, in the tens of millions of Euros, was staggering.

Kurt checked the clock over the microwave and leaped to his feet, cursing. He was due at the funeral in two hours, and he was not at all ready. Now he had a new dilemma. How could he keep a straight face at the funeral with this information? How could he act as if Mike's death was a tragic accident when it might have been an assassination? Mike had sent him the information for a reason. He had run out of people to trust, and he had circumvented all security channels.

Kurt scanned the room for a good place to stash the information. If whoever had killed Mike knew he had it, he wouldn't get much of a warning before they came after him. The only thing that made sense, he decided, was to keep the memory card on his body. That way he could react if someone came after it, and maybe buy himself enough time to figure out what else was there.

As a contingency, he created an encrypted partition on the laptop drive and copied all of the files into it. He secured it with AES 256-bit encryption, which as far as he knew, was still unbreakable, even by the NSA.

He stuffed the memory card into his pocket and raced upstairs to get dressed. Fifteen minutes later, the garage door rumbled open, and he eased his vintage silver Porsche 911 to the edge of the driveway. He looked both ways, and then took off with a screech.

Seven

KURT PUNCHED HIS ACCELERATOR AND shot across the highway into the church parking lot, skidding to a stop beside a shiny Mercedes SUV. Although he didn't like to think of himself as wealthy, it was hard to deny reality. His great grandfather, Augustus Vetter, had been an early pioneer in oil-extraction technology, and his patents had generated an enormous fortune for the family over the past hundred years. After that initial burst of wealth-generating effort, Augustus' descendants had diversified, going into a host of other businesses and eventually ending up as members of the political and financial elite. The result of this ancestral entrepreneurship was that Kurt and his family had more money than they could ever spend.

He climbed from his Porsche and gazed toward the cemetery, the same cemetery that held Amelia and Heidi. He looked away.

"Kurt!"

Kurt followed the call and saw his mom bustling through the door of the church and heading his way.

His father was right behind her, struggling to keep up. He strode toward them, but before he could get halfway, his mother closed the gap in a shuffling run.

She flew into his arms and threw her head against his shoulder, breaking into a fresh round of sobs. "Kurt—I'm so glad you made it," she gasped.

"I'm here, Mom." He patted her on the shoulder. Looking up, he nodded at his father. "Dad."

"Son."

Kurt disentangled himself from his mother and took a step back. After being on the road for so long, his sense of personal space was a bit out of adjustment. He held his hand out for his dad, who took it, before pulling him into an awkward embrace.

"Is everyone here?" Kurt asked, not knowing what else to say. His mother wiped a tear from the corner of her eye. *She isn't taking this well,* he observed. *But how could she?*

His father showed no emotion as usual. He stood ramrod straight, watching his wife blubber on, yet offering no condolences of his own. "We start in a few minutes," he said.

Kurt looked toward the church. At the same time, his father reached into his jacket pocket and extracted a pack of cigarettes—Camel, unfiltered. He held out the pack , and when Kurt shook his head, his father shrugged, knocked one out for himself, and lit up.

"Is everyone here?" Kurt asked again. Before his parents could answer, the door to the church swung open again and Amy, Mike's widow, stepped out. She had a determined smile on her face, which brightened a bit when she saw Kurt. She waved and started across the lot.

"Kurt," she said, as she approached. "Thank you so much for coming."

Kurt bit back the tears that were straining to break loose. He knew exactly what she was going through. "I'm so sorry, Amy," he said, opening his arms.

Amy melted into his embrace, molding herself to him. "He was so young, so full of life..." she sniffed. She was past the initial shock and probably well into the acceptance phase. The funeral was the worst part, everyone trying to comfort you, telling you everything would be all right. *Fuck them. They have no idea.*

Amy pulled back and gazed into Kurt's eyes. "This must hurt so much for you. Mike was such an amazing brother. I can't imagine what you're going through."

Kurt stared down at his feet, and then looked back at Amy. "Yeah." He couldn't think of anything else to say. He felt the same sense of loss, but unlike her, he was still in shock and acceptance was a long way off.

"Can I talk to you afterward?" he asked in a low voice, so no one else could hear.

"Sure." She gave him a quizzical look.

"Shall we?" his father interjected, gesturing toward the church.

Amy nodded. "Yes, I suppose so."

As a family, they entered the church. The funeral flew by, as they always did in Kurt's experience. Thankfully, Kurt didn't have to deliver a eulogy, although he would have done it if asked. Instead, Amy and his father carried out the duty, and admirably so.

The burial ceremony passed without incident. Mike was in the ground, and Kurt was the last remaining Vetter child. Immediately afterward, the family and guests regrouped and convoyed to Amy and Mike's house for the wake.

Kurt didn't stop to visit Amelia and Heidi's graves. That would come later, when he was alone.

The majority of the guests clustered in the living room, with some spilling onto the grand front porch that wrapped around the house. Mike and Amy's children, Emily and Philip, four and six respectively, wandered in and out of the proceedings, blissfully unaware of the full context.

"Uncle Kurt?" He turned and found Philip standing behind him dangling a miniature lacrosse stick from his little fist. His heart broke a little more as he gazed down at the little boy. He couldn't help but recall a vision of Heidi, several weeks before the accident, playing hide and seek with Mike's children. It had seemed so permanent at the time, as if the children had all the time in the world. He blinked the image away.

Kneeling down, he put himself eye to eye with Philip. His pain was no match for what this little man would go through over the next several years. "How are you, Phil?" he asked, holding out his hand.

Phillip took it and gave it a good shake. "Will you play with me, Uncle Kurt?"

"Sure! Do you have another stick?"

Philip beamed, obviously delighted to have someone to keep him company. "On the back porch!" He spun around and dashed towards the rear of the house. Kurt got back to his feet and took off in pursuit of his nephew. He hadn't had a chance to speak with Amy yet, and he figured this would help keep him occupied while he waited for an opportunity to do so.

He spent the next half hour tossing a ball back and forth with Philip. They had the backyard to themselves, stopping briefly to wave at Amy's sister Jessica, who was in charge of the children for the afternoon. The boy's skill with the ball impressed him. Deep down, he hoped Philip would channel the pain of his father's death into success on the game field. It had to go somewhere, after all.

The day was getting late, and Amy still hadn't shown her face. Kurt realized he couldn't hide out in the back yard with the six-year-old forever. It was time to go back inside and find her, and try to get some answers. "One more throw," he announced.

Phillip looked disappointed, but Kurt knew he would get over it.

"Why don't you go find your sister, see what she's doing," Kurt suggested. "I bet she'd like to play outside for a while, too." Philip's face brightened at the idea. He was still at the age when playing with his sister was an option. Kurt knew the boy had only a few more years before he developed a group of his own male friends, and that dynamic would be lost forever.

Once Philip was gone, Kurt made his way to the front of the house, searching the small knots of people for Amy's face. He was surprised and startled to find her sitting alone, staring into a cup of coffee, on a couch near the front door.

He took a seat beside her. "Amy," he said in his most respectful voice. "How are you holding up?"

She looked up, and Kurt realized she had been crying, not a lot, but enough to smudge her makeup. Amy dabbed at her eyes with a tissue and forced a wan smile onto her face. "I'll survive," she replied, blowing her nose. "Did you still want to talk?"

Kurt nodded. "Is now a good time?"

She shrugged. "I don't think any time is going to be good for a while."

Kurt shifted in his seat. She was right. "Okay, then... I was wondering if you noticed anything different about Mike before he died? Was he acting strange? Mood changes, late night phone calls, sudden trips, stuff like that?"

Amy blinked and shifted on the couch, putting some space between them. "Maybe, now that you ask. But that was Mike, you know?"

Kurt leaned in closer. "I'm not sure I understand..."

"Well, he was really moody in the last month or so, more than I've seen in a long time. Some nights he wouldn't come to bed until two or three in the morning." Her gaze wandered somewhere over Kurt's left shoulder, as if she was afraid to look him in the eyes. "Sometimes it seemed as if he was somewhere else entirely, as if he wasn't the man I had married." Her eyes met Kurt's again.

"Was it work?"

"It had to be. Things were going really well for us for a change..."

Kurt smiled. It was common knowledge in the family that Mike and Amy had had a stormy relationship from the start. "Mike told me you guys were going through a rough patch," he admitted. "Just before I left town."

Amy looked away again. "I figured. He never was very good at telling me what he really felt about things—about anything. He kept everything locked up so tight; it pained me to watch him sometimes. I guess it was because of work, but I don't know. Whatever it was, I had had enough. I told him he had to either figure out how to talk to me, to let me inside, or I was leaving." She tucked a stray strand of blond hair behind her ear and continued. "We found a therapist in Alexandria. It was tough at first, tougher than I expected. We both learned a lot. It turned out the problem was with both of us. We made real progress, damn it! However, after a few months—BAM! It was back to the old Mike. He was gone."

Kurt pressed harder. "Did he say anything about what he was doing at work? Any hints?"

Amy thought for a moment, shook her head. "Nothing. He was a stone wall."

Kurt rolled his shoulders and shifted on the couch. The tension of the day was killing him. "Was he traveling? Spending time alone?"

"Yes. He did take several trips. He wouldn't, or couldn't, say where. You know how he was about work."

Kurt filed that away for later. It wasn't unusual in itself. It wouldn't be a stretch for Mike to go out of the country on short notice. "Would you mind if I poked around his office?" he asked. He knew he was going out on a limb with that.

Amy didn't hesitate in her response. "No. Not at all." She got to her feet and led him through the house to Mike's office. He passed his parents on the way and noticed that his father appeared well on the way to a self-medicated oblivion, courtesy of Johnny Walker.

They walked down a long hallway in the southwest wing of the house. As they reached the ornate French doors leading to Mike's study, Amy stopped and turned to face him, stepping uncomfortably close. She stared up at Kurt's eyes for a long moment, and he had the feeling that she was waiting for him to kiss her. She needed someone to hold on to. He took a step back, hoping to defuse the awkwardness.

"Thanks, Amy. I'll leave it as I found it." The moment passed, and Amy was back to normal. She smoothed her hair and made a point of looking down the hall past Kurt, then she walked away.

Kurt went to the study and opened the door, stepping into his brother's inner sanctum. The feeling of being in Mike's personal space triggered a strong sense of déjà vu. It reminded him of an incident in junior high in which he had raided Mike's bedroom in search of his pot stash. He and a friend, eager to experiment, had concocted a theory in which Mike had a bag of weed hidden somewhere in his room. They had snuck in while Mike was at lacrosse practice and turned the room upside down. It all came to a disastrous ending, however, when Mike came home early and caught them. He could laugh about it now, but at the time, he had feared for his life. The feeling was the same now. He expected Mike to walk in behind him at any second and demand to know what he was doing.

The room was masculine, yet intimate, with a large mahogany desk stationed in front of a window overlooking the swimming pool. Bookshelves lined the rest of the walls. Titles ranged from cheap pulp paperbacks to elaborate treatises on global political systems. A fireplace covered part of the western wall, flanked by two leather wing chairs and a plush ottoman. Papers covered every available surface.

Kurt searched the desk first, and when he didn't find anything, he moved on to the rest of the room. A collection of framed photographs on one of the bookshelves drew his attention. They were a mix of family shots and pictures of people he didn't recognize. One picture in particular drew him in. It was his brother and two other people, a man and a woman. The picture was on a boat somewhere tropical. The subjects all wore wet suits, and a beaming Mike held a large fish in his arms. The picture was at least five or six years old judging by the lack of gray at Mike's temples. The woman in the picture was striking, he noted. She had dark, shoulder-length hair, piercing violet eyes and a long, slender neck. He picked up the frame and slid the picture out, searching for a date. Finding none, he replaced the picture, but not before mentally recording the image of the woman. Something about her intrigued him.

He spent the next ten minutes searching the rest of the office, flipping through books, soaking up what little he could discern of his brother's personal life. After two passes, he was satisfied he had seen all there was to see and let himself out of the office.

As soon as he reached the main gathering, he decided it was time to leave. The memory card was burning a hole in his pocket. He couldn't focus, and he wasn't ready to grieve. He made his rounds, saying his goodbyes. His mother made him promise to stop by the next day, and he reluctantly agreed.

As he approached the door, his mind a jumble of conflicting emotions, Kurt heard an unfamiliar voice call his name. He stopped and turned.

An older man was striding toward him with a

serious line drawn on his mouth. The man was dressed in a charcoal suit, crisp white shirt, and a red tie with faint charcoal accents. He screamed Agency. He moved with an easy grace, the body language of a man who was very comfortable with himself and the world around him. He behaved almost aristocratically, looking around as if he was a lord surveying his subjects.

They shook hands, and the man introduced himself. "Jack Carson. Your brother worked in my division."

Kurt's heart skipped a beat. "Uh...nice to meet you," he replied with as much indifference as he could muster.

"I wanted to say how sorry I am for your loss," Jack continued. "Mike was an outstanding member of the agency family. We're scrambling without him."

"Thank you." Kurt wanted to get away. He felt cornered, on the defensive.

Jack moved in closer, so close Kurt could smell his aftershave and the faintest trace of pipe tobacco on his breath. "It's tragic the way Mike died," Jack continued. "Were the two of you close?"

"Uh, yeah." Kurt glanced at the door.

"I don't mean to sound insensitive," Jack said, "but had you been in contact with him recently?"

Before the words were out, Kurt knew exactly where Jack was going with his line of questions. He took a step back, injecting some much-needed space between himself and the old spy. "No. We hadn't spoken in months. I was out of the country."

"Ah. That's right. It's been a bad year for you as well, hasn't it? I'm sorry for the loss of your family.

Positively tragic."

All of Kurt's instincts were screaming for him to get away as fast as possible. It took every bit of self-control he possessed to smile. "Thank you."

Jack's expression seemed to soften. "Thank you for speaking with me, Kurt." He fished in his pocket and extracted a card, which he pressed into Kurt's palm. "Please call me if you think of anything, night or day."

Kurt slid the card into his pocket. He did not intend to call this man, at least not until he figured out how he was connected to Mike's death. "Thanks."

"Any time. I mean it," Jack repeated.

Kurt gave a quick nod and slipped out the front door. He was parked a block down the street, and a minute later he was behind the wheel, accelerating away from his brother's house. He had a decision to make, and he had to make it fast. Jack Carson was not at Mike's house out of the kindness of his heart.

He was looking for information, and Kurt had a bad feeling he had provided it.

Eight

ON THE WAY BACK TO his office, Jack Carson picked up his phone and dialed Helen's secure line. She picked up on the first ring. "Helen here."

"It's Jack. I think I found out where our data went."

"Really?"

"Yeah. Vetter's brother, Kurt. I just got back from the wake. You should have seen the look on his face when I introduced myself. Like a deer in the headlights!"

"Are you sure?"

"No doubt. I had the idea this morning while I was getting ready to come over here. Did you know his brother was an analyst at the agency?"

"Really? No, I didn't know that." Helen's keyboard clattered in the background as she checked Kurt's records. "Hmmm."

Jack gave her a moment to peruse the file, packing and lighting his pipe to fill the void. He cracked a window to allow the smoke to escape.

"It says here he's somewhere in South America."

"The file is wrong. He's here, in Fairfax."

Jack came to a line of traffic stopped at a light and drifted into the right lane for his turn. "I want surveillance on the brother," he ordered. "Set up a 'sneak and peak' on his house, get his phone records, the works."

"I'm on it," Helen responded. "I'll have Mason hit his house as soon as possible."

The act of performing a 'sneak and peek' on a citizen was technically illegal, but the agency did it all the time. The ongoing surveillance, on the other hand, was a little trickier. Jack had the authority to order surveillance on anyone for up to twenty-four hours, as long as he was able to justify the target was a national security threat. After that, he had to petition a Foreign Intelligence Surveillance judge for a warrant.

"Good. I'll be there in about..." he checked his watch, "fifteen minutes." He flipped his phone shut and dropped it in the tray between the seats. The most important thing now was to verify that Kurt Vetter had the stolen information, and if he did, eliminate him and all traces of the files. That could only happen, Jack knew, if his team acted fast. He frowned, anger surging through his body, as he recalled Mike's betrayal. He had wasted two years grooming Mike to succeed him, two years of his life he would never get back. He scowled. *Ungrateful prick.*

A few miles down the road, Jack saw the top floors of the CIA complex poking through the trees. He smiled. Soon he would be moving to a much larger office, in downtown Washington. The country would see him as a hero, a man who had the courage and fortitude to eliminate a grave existential threat. He had no doubt of this, and the knowledge bolstered his confidence in his decisions. Despite appearances, he wasn't doing this for himself. No, this was for the country, for all of the people who had fought and suffered during the Cold War. Jack believed, and he had seen no evidence to the contrary, that he was the last true patriot.

He slowed at the entrance to the facility and retrieved his badge from his breast pocket. As his window came down, the air conditioning of his Lexus kicked in harder as it fought the sweltering humidity.

"Afternoon, Mr. Carson," the guard said. Jack had been coming to this facility for so long the guards knew him by face alone. Still, they had to do their jobs.

"Afternoon, Rich," Jack replied with a grin. He handed over his badge.

The guard, a trim Hispanic man in his early forties, took Jack's badge and compared it to his face. At the same time, sensors probed his car from beneath, analyzing it for explosive residues, radiation sources, and a host of other contraband deemed detrimental to the agency. Rich swiped Jack's badge through a portable card reader and the light turned green, indicating the badge was authentic.

"Have a nice afternoon, sir." Rich returned the badge.

"You too, Rich," he responded. He pushed the button controlling the driver's side window, sealing out the heat and restoring his climate-controlled bubble.

Nine

KURT PULLED INTO HIS DRIVEWAY and came to a stop a few inches from the garage door. He killed the engine, but remained in the driver's seat, lost in thought. All thoughts of the funeral were gone as he pondered the strange discussion with Mike's boss. Kurt had a gnawing feeling about the man. Something about him screamed danger. Something he couldn't quite identify.

"Screw it." He got out of the car and went into the gloomy house, heading straight for his computer. This time, instead of picking through files at random, Kurt typed in Jack Carson's name along with Mike's. Right away, he got three hundred results, ranked according to the frequency of the words within the documents. Fifteen documents contained both names. Kurt chose this subset and started reading.

An hour later, he sat back and took what felt like his first breath in days. This was bigger than he could handle alone. Despite his reservations, his only option was to trust his brother. He had to see Amanda Carter.

Kurt switched over to a web browser. He opened up Orbitz and initiated a search for an open-ended ticket from DC to Heathrow Airport, leaving as soon as possible. Three seats were available. He chose the one leaving at nine o'clock.

It was only six. That meant he had an hour and a half to get to the airport, maybe two if he got lucky with security and traffic. Dulles was only a half-hour away, but Northern Virginia traffic was notoriously unpredictable. He dashed upstairs and pulled his old travel bag from the master closet. He unzipped it and threw it on the bed. With practiced efficiency, he gathered two shirts, two pairs of pants, several pairs of underwear, a light jacket, and his shaving gear. Discarding all pretense of efficient packing, he dumped everything into the bag and zipped it shut

He grabbed the bag and raced back downstairs, killing the lights on the way. After a quick check of the locks, he took off.

~ * * *~

Helen Bartholomew yawned. She had been working since six o'clock in the morning and was sick and tired of staring at her computer screen. She rubbed the bridge of her aquiline nose, pushing her glasses up high on her forehead. A nasty migraine was begging to brew somewhere between her temples.

Her computer beeped and a message flashed on the screen. "Hmm... what's this?" She opened the message.

Vetter, J. London Heathrow. 0200Z. Read More?

She clicked on the 'Read More' link, and the

message expanded, listing the details of Kurt Vetter's ticket purchase.

She grinned. *Now this is more like it.* One of the wonderful benefits of working inside Langley was the direct tie-in with the real-time data collection efforts run by the NSA and the FBI. Helen had free rein to conduct analysis against this endless stream of data as it coursed through the arteries of the various intelligence networks, picking and choosing items of interest. Technically, she was unable to monitor traffic originating from within the United States, but since Kurt's flight terminated in the United Kingdom, she had full access.

She dialed Jack's number.

"This is Jack," she heard, in stereo. She swiveled around. Jack was standing right behind her, coat in hand.

She dropped her phone back into the cradle. "You were right. It looks like our boy is taking a trip. No return date." Helen rolled to the side and Jack leaned in to read the message.

After reading, he straightened to his full height and smiled. "I knew it. I want Mason on that flight."

"No problem." Helen's fingers flew across the keyboard, and a moment later, she looked up. "Done." She had placed Mason three seats behind Kurt.

"Good," Jack said. He took a seat on the edge of Helen's desk. "We need to find out where he's going. He must be meeting someone."

Helen shrugged. "It must be someone he trusts. Someone both he and Mike know."

"Yeah, but London? Can you run a search to cross-index all current and former agency employees connected to Mike who may be stationed over there?"

Helen bit her lip as she pondered the most effective search criteria. "Sure," she said, turning to the keyboard and entering the first query that came to mind. Zero results.

Jack got up and paced around the room. "Okay. That rules out someone on our side. It's got to be someone else then, another agency maybe?"

"Maybe it's the British?" Helen suggested.

Jack stopped pacing. "Interesting idea. The British." He drew the word out.

Helen's phone rang. "Mason," she said, indicating the caller ID. She picked it up.

"Hey, Mason."

"What's this about London?" Mason asked.

"Vetter is moving. You're on the nine o'clock flight."

Mason groaned. "Damn it! Let me talk to Jack."

"Sure. He's right here." She handed the phone to Jack. "He wants to speak with you."

Jack put the phone up to his ear. She watched his eyes narrow as he listened. Mason was probably complaining about the last minute posting.

He let him bitch for a good ten seconds before cutting him off, "Mason! Stop! Get your ass on that plane and take care of this guy. We'll cover things here."

After hanging up, Jack turned back to Helen. "I've got to make some calls. Let's talk again in an hour."

Helen acknowledged him with a grunt. She had already shifted her focus back to the national databases and was busy searching for the London connection.

Ten

A S USUAL, THE SHORT-TERM parking at Dulles was filled to capacity. Mason put his car in the blue long-term lot, and climbed onto the bus for the long ride to the British Airways terminal. He barely recalled the drive to the airport, having kept one eye on his phone and one eye on the road the entire time. Helen had been busy transmitting a wealth of information to him, including multiple pictures of Kurt Vetter as well as lists of his known contacts in London along with hotels and restaurants he had frequented in the past, all based upon information gleaned from his credit card records.

The bus slowed to a stop at the main terminal. Mason hefted his bag onto his shoulder and climbed out to the curb. Since he only had one piece of carry-on luggage, he proceeded straight to the security line, which wound through the main terminal like a coiled snake.

Much to his surprise, he spotted Kurt Vetter right away; twenty feet ahead, Vetter stood patiently, waiting to go through the security checkpoint. Mason sent a quick message to Helen informing her he had acquired his target. The line surged forward. Mason dug his passport out of his breast pocket. His boarding pass was stored in his phone. He was traveling as Max Pearson, a name close enough to his own that it wouldn't be difficult to remember if pressed.

The line shuffled forward again. In front of him, a young girl, maybe three or four, smiled up at him. Mason gave her a covert wave, sending her squealing for cover behind her mother's long legs. The girl tugged on her mother's hand and pointed at Mason. Although Mason knew he wasn't attractive by conventional standards, he felt he had a way with women of all ages with his quick sense of humor and easy smile that made them melt.

The girl's mother finally turned toward him to appease her daughter. Mason noted she wasn't wearing a ring on her left hand.

"Excuse me, sir," she said with a mischievous smile. "My daughter says you look like a man on TV."

Mason grinned and gave a hearty chuckle. "Don't I wish!" He held out his hand. "I'm Max."

The woman blushed. "I'm Carol. Where are you traveling today?" she asked.

"London. And you?"

"Los Angeles."

Mason knelt down. "And who, may I ask, are you?" he said to the little girl.

When the child didn't answer, her mother said, "Ruthie," making the little girl shriek in delight.

The line lurched forward again. They were almost at the point where they would separate into individual security lanes, and for a moment, Mason thought he had lost his target. He found him a second later, on the other side of the security checkpoint. He had bent to tie his shoes.

"Have a good trip," he told Carol and Ruthie. On any other day, he would have played the situation out, seeing where it would lead, but not this time.

"You too, Max. It was nice meeting you." Carol gave him a look as if she was about to say something, but then seemed to change her mind.

"Likewise." Traveling to the United Kingdom with weapons was dicey on a good day, so Mason had arranged to meet with an agency contact on the other side to retrieve a new side arm. It wasn't worth the trouble to try to carry one through security, despite what the movies showed, and he didn't want to travel under diplomatic cover either. This trip was strictly off the books.

On the other side of the checkpoint, he stopped to put his shoes back on. He glanced to his right and caught Carol's eye again. He gave her a quick wink, and then turned his attention back to Kurt, following him to the AeroTrain platform.

The departure gate was located on the B concourse, less than a five-minute ride away. Mason took a seat directly across from Kurt. He gave him a quick grimace of mutual suffering as the train accelerated away from the main terminal. Once they reached the concourse and exited the train, he dropped back in the crowd to give Kurt some breathing room.

They were departing from gate five, just a few minutes' walk from the trains. As far as Mason could tell, Kurt was traveling alone. This was what he expected, given the single ticket purchase, but anything was possible in a situation such as this.

Kurt stopped short in the middle of the concourse, causing a momentary traffic jam as people reacted to the sudden obstacle in their path. Mason ducked into a book kiosk and feigned interest in the bestseller rack while watching Kurt out of the corner of his eye.

Turning in a circle, Kurt appeared to be looking for something. *What the...?* Mason tried to follow his gaze. Kurt suddenly took off toward a bank of public computer terminals. Mason checked the time on his phone. Boarding call was still twenty minutes away.

As he watched, Kurt pulled out his wallet, extracted a credit card, swiped it through the card reader on the machine, and began typing.

Mason dialed Helen. She answered before the first ring. "Yeah Mason. What is it?"

"Vetter's using a public computer terminal. Concourse B..." He strained to read the number posted above the computer. "Looks like number eleven. He used his credit card."

Helen breathed heavily on the other end. "I've got it."

Mason waited, expecting her to say something else. When she didn't, he prompted, "Is there anything I need to know?"

"No. He's in an encrypted browser session. I can't read his traffic yet. It'll take a little while to figure out what he's doing..."

"Damn."

"Is that all?" Helen asked. She sounded frazzled.

Mason scratched his chin thoughtfully. "Yeah. For

now."

"Okay. Talk to you on the other side."

He ended the connection and pocketed his phone. Kurt was scribbling something on a piece of paper, which he then folded and shoved into his pocket.

A moment later, he finished whatever he was doing at the computer, pushed his chair back, and stood. With a quick glance around the concourse, he headed for the departure gate.

Barely able to constrain his curiosity, Mason fell in behind him. He had a bad feeling this was going to be a long assignment.

Eleven

HEATHROW TERMINAL FIVE WAS A zoo. Everywhere Kurt looked, there were people, some coming, some going, all sharing the same haggard, impatient look of air travelers the world over. In a previous life, Kurt had traveled through Heathrow for both personal and business reasons more times than he cared to remember. Right behind San Francisco International, it was his favorite airport in the world, partly because the United Kingdom looked and felt like home, while at the same time was different enough that he felt like he had really gone somewhere.

Contrary to his initial fears, customs had proven uneventful. "Quite the world traveler," the laconic customs agent had commented as she flipped to the back page of his passport and stamped it with a resounding *Ka-Chunk!*

Kurt slung his bag over his shoulder and set off toward a dark blue sign indicating the Piccadilly tube stop. The Piccadilly line connected the airport with central London, and from there, to the rest of the city. He had a hotel reserved in the West End, right down the street from the Cavendish Hotel, where he usually stayed.

As he strolled toward the exit, he pulled a small slip of paper from his pocket and unfolded it. The paper was blank except for Amanda Carter's London telephone number. He had looked it up while at Dulles, after having forgotten to do so in his frantic rush to get to the airport.

As he tucked the paper back in his pocket, his fingertips brushed the edge of his mobile phone, and he remembered that he had one more stop to make before he got on the train. He craned his head around and spotted a Vodafone kiosk a few dozen yards down the concourse.

"Hello, sir," the young woman behind the counter said with a smoky south-Asian accent. She looked to be in her late twenties, with large brown eyes and a perky, upturned nose. Lustrous black hair cascaded to her shoulders, and she wore a brightly-colored sari. A small red gem, or bindi, pasted slightly above and between her eyebrows completed the outfit.

"Hey," Kurt said, fumbling his phone from his pocket. "I need a prepaid SIM card."

"Is your phone unlocked sir?"

"It is."

"Will you need data connectivity during your stay?"

Kurt didn't know, but decided it couldn't hurt. "Sure."

"How much would you like to start with?" the woman asked, pointing at a laminated price sheet on the edge of the counter.

Kurt picked it up and studied the rates. He had no idea how much he would need. "Do you take US dollars?" he asked, flustered.

"We do." She beamed. "We take most currencies."

"Let's start with two hundred, then." Kurt dug out his wallet and pulled out two crisp hundred-dollar bills. He placed them in the small plastic tray on the counter.

"Right." She scooped them up, and the currency disappeared into her till.

While she programmed his new SIM card, Kurt removed the back of his phone and ejected the battery. He scraped out the existing SIM with his fingernail and stuffed it into the back of his wallet for safekeeping. Once the new SIM was ready, the clerk snapped it from its plastic frame and handed it over.

Kurt thanked her and inserted it into his telephone.

"You can see your number by pressing Menu, six, three," the clerk informed him.

Kurt followed her instructions and verified his new number. Satisfied all was working, he thanked her and resumed his trek to the tube stop.

~ * * *~

Mason loitered at a newsstand and thumbed through the latest issue of the International Herald Tribune. He yawned and stole a casual glance over at Kurt, who was fifty feet away at a phone kiosk.

So far, so good. Upon touchdown, Mason had turned on his phone and sent an encrypted text message to Helen. She had replied right away, telling him there was no news on her end. He noticed movement down the concourse. *Shit. What's he doing now?*

Mason folded his paper and broke into a brisk walk as he trailed Kurt down the concourse. There were enough people milling about that losing his subject was a distinct possibility, one he didn't want to test.

Mason had spent copious amounts of time in London over the years, to the point that it felt almost like a second home to him. He could even pull off a passable London accent in a pinch, a talent that was usually only good for party tricks, but one he felt could prove extremely useful on this assignment.

He followed Kurt onto the tube platform, and when the train arrived, he took a prime seat in the next car with a clear view of Kurt's movements and those of the people around him. As the train approached the rough and tumble outskirts of London proper, his phone buzzed. Helen.

Mason placed the phone close to his left shoulder for a moment until he felt a subtle vibration through his fingertips. Then he ran the top of his index finger over the camera on the backside, triggering the built-in fingerprint reader to unlock the device.

His phone was a new model, styled to look like a common smart phone. It contained an advanced radio frequency identification chip which, in concert with a similar chip embedded deep underneath the muscle of his left pectoral, ensured the phone was useless if lost or stolen. In order to access any encrypted information, he was required to make a close proximity connection between the chip inside the phone and the chip embedded within his body. Mason still didn't like the idea of walking around with a chip buried inside of him, but the idea of life without access to all of the information provided by his phone was even less palatable. It was a tradeoff he was willing to make—for now. Mason looked at the screen. He had an email, containing Kurt Vetter's hotel information. He recognized the hotel, having stayed there once himself. He put the phone back in his pocket and dug back into the Trib.

~ * * *~

Kurt stifled a yawn as the train pulled into the Piccadilly Circus tube station. He needed coffee, and he needed it now. But first, he wanted to try Amanda Carter.

He pulled the paper from his pocket, took out his phone, and punched in her number. "Here goes nothing," he said under his breath. He pressed Send.

The phone only rang once before a woman answered. "Hello?" He couldn't tell for certain if it was an American or British accent, it was so fast, but his gut said American.

He cleared his throat. "Uh, hello. This is Kurt Vetter."

There was a moment of silence, then, "I'm sorry, but you've reached the Bull and Gate Pub. You must have the wrong number." The line went dead.

Definitely American. Confused, he double-checked the number he had dialed against the slip of paper. He had dialed correctly. Then it came to him. *She can't talk on this line.*

He dug through his bag for his London city guide. He opened it and found the Bull and Gate Pub in the index. He flipped to page fifty-six and noted the address. He snapped the guide shut and stuffed it back in his bag. Hurrying outside, he flagged down the first taxi he saw.

"The Bull and Gate pub. Three eighty-nine Kentish Town Road."

"Right."

The taxi driver launched them into the thick morning traffic, mashing Kurt back into the seat and sending his bag tumbling from his grasp.

~ * * *~

At the Piccadilly exit, Mason stared in disbelief as Kurt closed the taxi door, and it pulled away from the curb. "Shit!" he cursed. He had only been on the ground an hour, and he was already in danger of losing his target. With one eye on Kurt's taxi, he flagged down his own. He wrenched the door open, threw his overnight bag across the back seat, and yelled, "Follow that taxi!"

The driver, a diminutive Sikh with an enormous Turban, turned to him and said, "Which one, sir?"

Mason looked over the Sikh's shoulder and saw to his dismay that there were now dozens of black taxis jostling for position on the street. He had no way to tell. He popped his head out of the taxi window, trying to get a better view. It was no use. He had lost his target.

"Just drive," he said, climbing back in. "That way." He pointed in the direction he thought Kurt had gone. For the moment he could only drive, relying on an electronic intercept from Helen to help reacquire his target. It was possible, but not probable that the intercept would occur before Jack found out how badly he had screwed up. His only other option would be to try to intercept him at his hotel, but if Kurt were as smart as Mason thought he was, he wouldn't go there. He'd hole up somewhere else, somewhere no one knew about.

No. Waiting was not an option.

Twelve

HELEN RUBBED HER EYES AND tossed back the dregs of coffee that had been cooling beside her keyboard for the past two hours. She was seventeen hours into a nine-hour shift, and she was feeling every second of it.

She scrolled her mouse pointer with her index finger, flitting through the latest intelligence intercepts on the Russian Federation, looking for anything out of the ordinary, anything that would indicate a problem with the operation. She couldn't find anything.

Jack would be happy about that, and when Jack was happy, Helen was happy. It was like a marriage in that respect, albeit a severely dysfunctional one. Jack could be an absolute tyrant, she had learned early on, but when he was getting his way, he was an angel. At least that's what she told herself.

She got up and stretched, running through her usual routine of desk-side yoga poses to get her blood flowing. Her ass was numb from sitting so long, and she had a mean crick in her neck. The yoga wouldn't solve everything, but it would help. Sleep was still a long way off.

Out of the corner of her eye, she noticed a yellow indicator flashing on her monitor. It was one of her software agents—programs that continuously scanned a host of government databases, looking for interesting information. She slid back into her chair and double-clicked on the alert, expanding it to fill her entire screen.

"Hmmm." The message was only a few lines long. According to the header, it had come from the Rapier system, the big brother to the FBI's infamous Carnivore. Rapier, sent into production only a year before, made Carnivore look like a child's video game. It was a quantum leap forward, literally, as it relied on cutting-edge quantum computing techniques which allowed it to ingest and process almost infinite quantities of data in near real-time. That meant that what she was reading was only seconds, or at the most, minutes.

The message said:

```
<Result>
<NameRef>
Kurt Vetter
</NameRef>
<Mobile>
<Loc>
London, UK
</Loc>
<Time>
07272015T0800Z
</Time>
</Mobile>
```

```
<detail>
124AX7FF
</detail>
</Result>
```

It was gibberish to the untrained eye, but to Helen it was like finding a needle in a haystack of needles. The Rapier system had intercepted a mobile telephone call containing the words 'Kurt Vetter' at eight o'clock London time. The string of text in the detail section indicated there was more information about the call available.

"Gotcha!" Despite her fatigue, she couldn't help the grin that lit up her face. She picked up her secure telephone and dialed Mason.

He answered on the first ring. "Mason here."

"It's Helen. I've got something for you."

There was traffic noise in the background, the distinctive high-low warble of a UK ambulance somewhere nearby. Helen clicked into a different window on her system and watched as a red dot representing Mason crawled through downtown London.

"Vetter called someone in London. I'll have the address for you in a second."

"Good..." She couldn't help but notice the note of relief in his voice.

Helen double-clicked on the *More* link, and a new window opened, listing the owners of the phones involved in the call and their addresses, as well as a brief synopsis summarizing each party in the call.

"It looks like he contacted someone named Amanda Carter. He spoke for ten seconds before disconnecting."

"Interesting. Any background—"

"Hold on a second," she said, cutting him off. She clicked on the second page of Amanda's information.

"It says here she's attached to the embassy."

"What do you mean?" Mason asked. "Is she one of us?"

"Patience, Mason," she said, nearly losing her own.

There was a long list of hyperlinks under Amanda's dossier, but they were all colored red, and she couldn't click on any of them.

"This is strange..."

"What?"

"I don't know. I can't get into any of this woman's background. She's in our system, but I don't have permission to access her files."

Helen took Amanda's information, as much as she was able to collect, and pasted it into a new message. She put Mason's name at the top. "I'm sending you her address and as much background as I have. You'll have to do this the old-fashioned way. I've also got a trace set on the mobile that Vetter used. That's on the way as well."

She clicked Send, and the information shot out across the Atlantic.

"I'll keep digging on this end, but first I have to take this to Jack," she added, as she sent Amanda's dossier to the color printer behind her.

"Sure."

Helen heard Mason's phone beep as it received the information.

"Got it," he said.

"Are you still in contact?"

Mason went silent. "I had a little problem..."

"Goddamn it, Mason! What happened? No—screw it. Don't tell me. Just fix it! The trace should be active now. That should help."

She knew Mason wouldn't bother explaining. It didn't matter how he had lost his target, only that he had. "Thanks. I've got him on my screen now."

"Good. I'm off to brief Jack. I'll let you know as soon as I find something else."

"Same here." The line went dead. Helen sucked in her breath and got to her feet.

This woman, whoever she was, could prove to be a major problem for all of them.

Thirteen

KURT EXITED THE CAB AND stood on the curb in front of the Bull and Gate. The building was old. *Victorian-old*, he thought, *maybe older*. The door and the trim on the exterior were bright blue, like the picture in the tour guide. Up close, though, it was obvious the building was ancient. The paint, peeling in places, was thick and dull; the palm-sized panes of window glass were shot through with whorls and imperfections, obscuring his view of the interior.

As his taxi melted back into the snarled traffic, he surveyed his surroundings. It was a beautiful London morning, and the sidewalks were full of pedestrians enjoying the unseasonably warm temperatures. Although it was only ten thirty in the morning, the pub was open for business. He pushed through the heavy wooden door and stepped into the cool, dark interior.

The first thing he noticed was the stale odor struggling to compete with the thick smell of decades—no—centuries of fried meals. His stomach rumbled, whether from hunger or disgust, he wasn't sure. His last meal had been eight hours earlier, so he suspected it was a bit of both.

The pub was empty except for a few locals, identifiable by their Manchester United football jerseys. They sat at one end of the bar engrossed in a match playing on a large flatscreen television. At the other end of the bar was a young tourist couple, probably American from their dress. They were speaking to each other in hushed tones, holding hands, oblivious to the world.

Kurt made his way to the back of the pub, searching for the restrooms. He pissed, washed his hands, and splashed water on his face. Checking his reflection in the mirror, he traced his fingers along the bags under his eyes, not surprising considering he had been on the go for close to seventy-two hours. He splashed some more water on his face and then left the bathroom.

As he made his way down the hall, he saw a woman standing near the front door. Her back was to him, and she appeared to be checking her watch. She hadn't been there when he entered. Dressed in a black pencil skirt and white blouse, she had shoulder-length auburn hair and a tight athletic build. Kurt raised his eyebrows, intrigued. *Amanda?*

He was almost to the woman when he felt a hand brush his elbow. "Kurt?" a female voice asked.

Kurt turned. It was the woman from the picture in Mike's study. He shot a glance at the woman near the door. She was hugging a man who had just entered the pub.

Turning back to the woman who had spoken to him, the first thing he noticed was her eyes. They were deep pools of violet, drawing him in and locking his gaze to hers. He had never seen such a color before and wondered for a moment whether they were real, but then he recalled the picture. *They were real.* The next thing he noticed was her height. In the picture, standing beside Mike, she had appeared much shorter, but in person, she was at least five-foot-seven. She wore blue jeans, strappy, black open-toed shoes with a slight heel, and a blouse that showed off her toned arms.

"Maybe," he said, feigning confidence. There was a reason Kurt had gone into analysis at the CIA rather than operations. He had never been good at thinking on his feet, always coming up with the perfect witty response long after the moment had passed.

"Come with me," she implored, grabbing his hand.

He had no choice but to follow as she dragged him down the hallway he had come through. She led him through the kitchen and into the alley that ran behind the pub. Parked just outside the door was a deep blue, almost black Mini Cooper club wagon. She pulled a set of keys from her pocket and remotely unlocked the doors. "Get in."

Kurt complied, not sure where this was headed.

As soon as the doors closed, the woman put the car in gear. They rocketed down the alley and back into traffic; the tiny engine screamed as she pushed it to the red line before each shift.

"You must be Amanda," he said.

"Uh huh. You look like your brother," she responded, shooting him a quick sidelong glance as she darted through the slow-moving traffic. Kurt thought he looked nothing like Mike, and he had never heard the comparison before, but who was he to argue?

She turned hard to the left, blowing a traffic signal and nearly flattening a lackadaisical pensioner. She pushed the car harder, leaving a wake of blaring horns behind them. Kurt held on for his life. He was beginning to wonder if getting in the car was the best decision he could have made.

"Where are we going?" he asked.

She didn't respond, instead focusing on the road ahead.

She made two more quick turns, and then, with a furtive glance in the rearview mirror, pulled over to the side. "Get out."

Kurt didn't really feel he had a choice. He popped the door and climbed out. They had stopped at a small park that ran down to the bank of the Thames, and Amanda was striding toward the water's edge, leaving him behind. She was heading for an ornate iron bench. He hurried to catch up, reaching her as she got to the bench. "Hold on!" he yelled, putting a hand on her elbow.

She spun away and shot him a withering glare that bore through him like a violet laser. He yanked his hand back as if he had been shocked. "Don't touch me," she said in a low, threatening tone.

He took a step back. "What the hell is going on here?" he demanded.

"You tell me," Amanda shot back. "You're the one who called me."

"Huh?"

"Don't 'huh' me! Why are you here? What kind of shit has your brother gotten himself into this time?"

She doesn't know, Kurt realized with a start. *She*

has no idea Mike is dead. The thought also crossed his mind that his brother and this woman had some sort of history, but he pushed it back. *Later.* "Mike's dead," he blurted.

The transformation was instantaneous. It was as if she had been punched in the gut. All of the fire and bluster disappeared in an instant. She put her hand on the park bench behind her and sank down on it. "Dead? Mike?"

"Yeah. A few days ago." He watched her face. Her emotions appeared genuine. *Just how are Mike and this woman connected?*

She stood and stepped close, taking up all of the space between them. Staring into his eyes, she asked, "Who killed him?" Her brief flash of grief was gone, replaced by seething anger.

The question caught him off guard. The official cause of death was robbery, or more specifically, a carjacking gone wrong. That she assumed someone had killed Mike spoke volumes about her history with his brother. "I've got some ideas," Kurt answered.

"Let me guess. He told you to get in contact with me in case of his death."

He nodded slowly, caught off guard by the anger in her eyes. "How did you—"

"That figures. I was always bailing his ass out of tight spots," she said with a trace of melancholy. "Your brother—"

"So you worked together?" he asked, interrupting.

She looked away. "In a manner... it's complicated." He raised an eyebrow. "Let's sit."

Settled on the bench beside him, Amanda remained silent for a moment, watching the sluggish river curl by. Kurt sensed she needed some time, that she was still getting used to the news.

"How did it happen?" she asked, softer this time.

He gave her the official version of Mike's death, starting at the gas station and working his way up and through the funeral. He told her everything he knew, everything that is, except about the mysterious package. Talking through it seemed to make it more real. He had lived the aftermath, but somehow it had seemed, up to this point, like someone else's tragedy.

"So how did my name come up?" Her tone had shifted again, serious but no longer angry.

"First, why don't you tell me how you knew my brother," Kurt demanded, setting his jaw. He was prepared to walk away, to catch a cab, and go back to his hotel if she wasn't willing to give some information.

Amanda seemed to look through him. "You work for the same agency as your—"

"Worked," he corrected.

She cocked her head and focused her gaze. "Worked?"

"It's a long story." That she knew where he had worked, that she seemed to know an awful lot about him while he knew nothing about her, was getting on his nerves.

"Okay. Where was I? Your brother and I met a long time ago, in a different life."

He fidgeted on the bench and turned his head slightly to ensure they still had the park to themselves. They did, so he turned back to Amanda.

"Your brother and I had the opportunity to... ah... work together on several occasions."

"So you're agency?" he asked.

She didn't answer. He knew that meant no. Kurt was confused. His brother had been a CIA operative; he had been ever since he got out of college. Then it struck him; she worked for another government.

"Who do you work for then?"

Amanda gave him a thin smile in response. "That's enough about me. How did you get my name?"

He realized she wasn't going divulge her employer, not yet, at least. He didn't like the imbalance of information, but he no choice but to run with it and see where it led. He owed it to Mike. He pulled the memory card from his pocket and held it up between his index finger and thumb so she could see it.

"And that is?"

He swallowed. He could be handing classified information to an enemy agent for all he knew. "I'm not sure exactly, but from what I've seen, it contains classified CIA personnel files, documents describing some pretty crazy war-gaming scenarios, a bunch of financial information, and last, but not least, a note saying I should find you, that you'd know what to do with it."

Amanda took the memory card and held it up, squinting. "Why didn't you take it to the agency?"

The question caught him off-guard, but the answer came surprisingly fast. "He was my brother. I trust him."

"You did the right thing." She pulled a smart phone from her pocket, flipped it over, and ejected the memory card with her thumbnail.

"Did I?" Kurt wasn't sure.

She paused with the card between her fingers and locked eyes with him. "Yes. You did." She slid the memory card into the phone. He waited as she navigated through the files on the phone; her delicate fingers danced across the device, paused, and then danced some more. As he watched, her eyes grew wide.

Finally, she looked back up at him. Her mouth was set in a grim line, and he thought she looked scared for the first time since he had met her.

"What is it?" he asked.

"This," she said, gesturing to the screen, "is crazy."

Kurt ran his fingers through his hair. "What do you mean? "

"This group Mike was working for—they're planning some sort of attack in Moscow, something big. What it is...? I can't tell. "

Kurt shook his head. "There's no way! Mike wouldn't get involved in something like that!"

Amanda's eyes bored into him, challenging him to provide some proof to the contrary. It all made sense, Kurt realized with a sinking feeling. He had been resisting the truth, afraid to submit to reality. All of his energy, his enthusiasm to catch Mike's killers, drained away. He slumped on the bench. "So what now?" Amanda shrugged and fiddled with the phone.

"We have to tell someone," Kurt suggested, realizing how absurd the words were as they left his mouth.

"I agree, but who? The CIA is out. Fucking spooks! You never know which side they're playing for." Amanda stared past him at the river. "The first thing we need to do is get the rest of these files decrypted. I've got a guy who can help."

Kurt perked up. "Can we trust him?"

"Absolutely."

"And then what?"

"We'll deal with that when we get there."

Kurt swallowed hard, not comfortable with the idea. His internal moral compass screamed at him to run to the embassy and hand over the data, to make it someone else's problem.

However, that was impossible; His brother had died to get this information to him. Now Kurt knew for sure his killers were the same people he had trusted with his life.

No. There has to be another way.

Fourteen

MASON WATCHED AMANDA'S MINI PULL away from the park, then checked his phone, again. Two dots, representing the tracers on Kurt and Amanda's phones, were moving in unison through central London, as Helen had said they would.

He breathed a sigh of relief and vowed he wouldn't be so sloppy next time. Losing his target was a rookie mistake, one that could jeopardize the entire operation.

As the Mini vanished around a hedgerow, he decided it was time to check in with the mother ship to spread the good news. He stepped out of the taxi and started dialing.

~ * * *~

Helen's phone rang, startling her.

"It's Mason," she announced to Jack as she answered.

"What's up, Mason?" she asked. "I've got Jack with me. I'm putting you on speaker."

Jack held up a finger. "Hold on a second." He closed Helen's office door and took a seat on the edge of her desk. "Okay. Go ahead." He closed his eyes and bowed his head, a habit Helen found highly annoying, yet was grateful for because it meant he was paying close attention.

Helen switched the phone to speaker and then leaned back in her chair and hooked her heels on the railing underneath the desk.

She heard Mason clear his throat before he said, "Vetter made contact with a woman, presumably Amanda Carter. They drove to a park on the Thames, where they spoke for about a half-hour. They just left, together."

Jack opened his eyes with a surprised look that mirrored her own.

"Did you recognize her?" Jack asked.

"No. I've never seen her before. I don't think she's from Langley." Helen knew that it was still possible that she had been at Langley at one time. It was also possible that one of the other alphabet-soup intelligence agencies running operations around the world employed her. NSA, DIA, NRO, even the FBI. It was a long list, and the people within the organizations moved around the community like ghosts.

"Damn..." Jack gazed at the map on her screen, but didn't appear to be really seeing it. He scratched the stubble on his jaw, then tugged on his earlobe. "We're watching them real-time from here," he added, almost as an afterthought.

"I figured—" A car roared by, blotting out Mason's voice for a moment.

"What was that Mason?" she asked. "We lost you for a second."

"Nothing."

Jack stood and pointed at the map. "I want to know where they're going and who this woman is. And I want to know yesterday."

"We'll get them," Helen said with more optimism than she felt. She forced a weak smile.

Jack looked at her with one eyebrow cocked. "Do you have anything else for Mason?"

"No."

"We'll talk to you soon, Mason." He bent across Helen and severed the connection.

Before she could suppress it, she yawned so hard her hearing fuzzed out for a second, and her vision faded to black. Embarrassed, she belatedly put her hand over her mouth.

Jack surprised her by saying, "I'm heading back to my office to catch a little shut-eye. I suggest you do the same."

Shocked, she gaped up at him, then quickly recovered her composure. "Okay." She felt like a zombie, so tired she couldn't think straight. She was liable to get someone killed while operating in this state.

"Keep your phone on," Jack tossed out as he left her office. "Just in case."

Everything seemed to be on track; everything that is, except for Kurt Vetter and Amanda Carter. Helen didn't like this. In her experience, the only time things were on track was right before they fell apart.

It would have to do for now. Sleep beckoned.

Fifteen

FISH COLDWELL TOOK A DRAG from his Marlboro Red, sucking the remains of the cigarette down to the filter in one fierce pull. He held the smoke in for a second, savoring the burn in his lungs, and then pursed his lips and exhaled like a dragon. He flicked the dead butt from the balcony and watched as it tumbled end over end before exploding in a shower of sparks on the street far below.

Rolling his head, he grimaced at the tightness deep in the muscles his neck, the chronic hint of pain that lurked just out of reach in the center of his back. *I'm too old for this...*

Fish was on the ground when the wall fell, when Perestroika exploded across the Soviet Bloc, razing the walls of Communism to the ground. He had experienced firsthand the dismissal of his life's work, the calculated indifference to the sacrifices he and others of his generation had made. It was for this reason he had joined up with Jack Carson—to finish the job for good.

He knew deep in his gut that Russia could never be

a free nation. From day one, the same players who had controlled the Soviet system had maneuvered themselves to take control in the new power vacuum. It was a classic case of 'meet the new boss, same as the old boss.' Starting in the early nineties, the Russian government had embarked on a privatization binge, shedding state businesses for pennies on the dollar. Then the mafia moved in, buying up all of the businesses and transforming them into transnational money machines. The Mafia knew the people wanted—no, needed—someone to tell them how to lead their lives.

Then, around the dawn of the millennium, things really kicked into high gear. A new nationalistic movement emerged. The Russian people were sick of poverty, sick to death of it, while the people in power longed for a return to the glory. From that point on, it was only a matter of time before the government reconstituted itself and reasserted control over the day-to-day aspects of life.

Knowing the long-term implications for his country, Fish had watched all of this unfold from the sidelines. Some within the United States government had welcomed the return to a world with two superpowers. They pined for the good old days of the Cold War when America had a single enemy rather than the constant barrage of insurgencies in third-world hellholes. What they didn't understand, and certainly didn't appreciate, was that the world had changed. Russia was but one of many new superpowers. China, Pakistan, India, and countless other small countries had exploded onto the international stage during the long hibernation of the Russian bear, and they were far more nimble than Russia could ever hope to be. Compounding that, they had legitimate bones to pick with their neighbors.

The problem, Fish had realized, was not Russia returning to superpower status. That was improbable. Russia had fallen too far and too fast to ever be more than a second-rate player. The real problem was that they had resources, including a sprawling nuclear arsenal, and in a bid for power, they could ally themselves with one of the new up-and-coming states and create something far more dangerous than the Soviet regime had ever been.

When Fish had pitched his idea to Jack, he framed it as an academic thought exercise, the sort of discussion old warriors shared over a beer. His instincts had been spot-on. Jack was in the same position, had the same concerns. He was on board before Fish could even complete his sales pitch. Russia as a nation was far too dangerous to exist. Elimination was the only option, elimination on a grand scale. It was the only option.

Fish pulled his smokes from his pocket and shook out another. He lit it with his dented titanium Zippo and turned to gaze upon the woman sprawled on his bed.

"Come back to bed, Alexy," the woman purred when she realized he was watching. Oksana, and everyone else in Moscow for that matter, knew him as Alexy Katadin, a wealthy expat businessman with money to burn and a bone to pick with the Moscow government. She lifted the sheets to give him a look at what he was missing, then ran a hand down her milky-white thigh and into the damp patch between her legs in a not-so-subtle invitation.

For a brief moment, Fish considered going another round with her, but truth be told, he was sore from fucking all night. More importantly, he had things to do. He and Magamod Gasanov had a meeting in two hours.

"Not now, Oksana," he said in flawless Russian. "Maybe later." She pouted for a moment, and then slipped from the bed and padded off toward the bathroom. Fish couldn't help but admire her perfect ass as she walked away from him. It was her best feature, after all. He felt a slight stirring in his loins. *Maybe I should fuck her again,* he considered. Then he shook his head, turned, and took another drag.

The toilet flushed, and Fish turned back to watch Oksana emerge from the bathroom. She looked different. She had brushed her hair and scrubbed the sleep from her face.

She came to him and draped her arms around his neck, fingernails teasing the skin at the base of his neck. She pressed her naked body against his. He felt himself twitch, but pushed her away. "I said, not now." He couldn't fault her for trying. He had promised her an enormous bonus for her services after all.

She put her hands on his cheeks, and then leaned in and pecked him on the lips. "Okay then. I will go."

Fish said nothing. His thoughts were already on his meeting with the Chechen.

Oksana went to the bed and scooped up her clothes. She slipped into her cocktail dress and pulled on her shoes, somehow making even such a simple motion look seductive. Her panties went into her purse. With one last smile, she let herself out of the apartment.

As the door clicked shut, Fish made for the shower. Oksana, unfortunately, would be his last dalliance before the big event. After his meeting with Gasanov, things would move very fast. His job for the day was to ensure the device was in place and that the Chechens understood how to operate it, then to get the hell out of town. He had a seven o'clock flight to Madrid, from where he planned to watch the fireworks. The bomb was set to detonate less than forty-eight hours from now.

The timing of the explosion was far from random. Fish had used every negotiating tactic in his book to convince the Chechens to wait until the sixteenth of July, the day when the entire leadership of the Russian Federation was in Moscow. Impatient bastards.

He scrubbed himself, washing Oksana's scent from his body. The hot water drilled needles in his back as he ran through a mental checklist. He finished his shower and stepped out, grabbing a thick terrycloth towel from the heated rack to dry himself.

Then he returned to his bedroom where he pulled a shiny black suit, a black shirt, and a pair of polished snakeskin cowboy boots from the closet. It was a carefully crafted image, designed to both intimidate and impress.

He dressed quickly, finishing off the uniform by slicking his hair back and wrapping a chunky Rolex Submariner around his right wrist. He did a quick turn in the mirror. Satisfied, he went to the bedside stand and retrieved his mobile phone. His meeting with Gasanov wasn't scheduled to start for another hour. *Plenty of time.*

Fish scanned the room one last time, and then headed for the door. This place, like most everything else in his life, was disposable. He had lived in the apartment for a little over two months. It was completely off the agency books, unknown even to Jack. That type of discretion was necessary when operating this far undercover. Even his agency phone, with its built-in beacon, was kept powered off when he got within a five-block radius of the building. In the event that something went wrong, he needed the ability to walk away, to deny any involvement if the shit hit the fan.

Fish took the elevator to the ground floor and exited into the secure basement, where he kept his black Mercedes E350. Twenty minutes later, he pulled up to a decrepit warehouse a few blocks from the Lubyanka prison in north-central Moscow. The warehouse was four-stories tall, covered in rust, and appeared abandoned from the exterior.

Almost before his tires stopped moving, a two-story door trundled open on rusty wheels. Fish blipped the gas, squirting through the door and into the cavernous space. Behind him, the doors rolled shut again, casting him into darkness.

He pulled forward a few yards, and then killed the ignition.

He saw four men. He knew that there were at least four more. That was how Magamod Gasanov worked. All of the men carried guns and had the bored, yet lethal, expression Fish had come to expect from private military contractors.

Fish took a deep breath and pasted a wide smile on his face. He opened the door and hoisted his bulk from the car.

Sixteen

MAGAMOD GASANOV EMERGED FROM A dim room at the far end of the warehouse and strode toward Fish. The heels of his boots clicked on the oil-stained concrete like a woodpecker on crack. "Alexy!"

At a hair over five-feet tall and a hundred and twenty pounds soaking wet, Gasanov looked more like an over-excited schoolboy than a battle-hardened Chechen rebel.

That was at a distance. Up close, it was an entirely different story. Bat-shit crazy about summed him up, Fish had decided long ago. Gasanov had a mysterious air about him that inspired fierce loyalty from his friends and an almost paralyzing fear from his enemies, of which he had many. Something wasn't right with him, something at the very core of his being. Looking into his eyes was like staring into a dark cave on a moonless night.

Gasanov had earned his reputation as a field commander during the second Chechen war in 1999. Once the fighting ended, and the Chechen drive for independence crumbled, he shifted focus and used his new influence to seize control of the majority of the criminal enterprises in his region, expanding his holdings to include arms trafficking, opium—mostly from Afghanistan—and prostitution. He also dabbled in low-level terrorism for hire, contracting his seasoned fighters to assist in the fight against the Americans in both Afghanistan and Pakistan. He was personally responsible for a large portion of the infamous foreign fighters present during the Iraq conflict.

Fish put a smile on his face and took a few steps forward, meeting Gasanov halfway. He slipped into his best Russian, and said *"Privet."*

Gasanov beamed, his tight little weasel teeth gleaming in the fluorescent light from above. "My friend!" he responded, in English. He put a hand on Fish's elbow, guiding him toward an enormous wooden crate.

"It is here," Gasanov said with a gleam in his eye. "I wanted to give you the honor of unwrapping our little present." *He's like a kid on Christmas morning,* Fish thought. He had never seen this side of the warlord before. Fish opened his mouth to protest, but Gasanov held up his hand.

"I insist. It is only fair that you participate in this momentous occasion. After all, we would not be here without your hard work."

Fish smiled a tight, efficient grin.

Gasanov nodded, then picked up a long pry bar leaning against the crate and handed it to Fish. He picked up a second one for himself.

Five minutes later, the men had broken the entire

crate away, revealing a battered metal box within. The box was eight feet long by four feet wide by three feet tall, olive green, and liberally stenciled in yellow Cyrillic glyphs. The universal symbol for radiation was plastered conspicuously on each side. Three bulky metal latches lined the edge closest to the men, with an additional latch on each end.

Gasanov wasted no time bending to the latches and undoing them one by one. Fish held his breath while Gasanov lifted the cover of the box. The two closest guards, cradling Kalashnikovs, took an involuntary step forward, unable to resist the mystery.

There it was.

Five feet long and cone-shaped, the warhead, a 150-kiloton Russian SS-20, was nestled in dense black protective foam. A sheaf of manuals and several bundles of wires hung from inside the lid of the crate.

"Pytor!" Gasanov barked. A nervous-looking man of about seventy shuffled forward and peered at the device. Fish hadn't met him before.

"Acceptable?" Gasanov asked in Russian.

The old man extracted a Geiger counter and waved it over the weapon, checking the meter and making notes on a small note pad as he did so. He unscrewed a plate on the top center of the device and examined some internal electronics with a small handheld computer.

He hummed while he worked, some sort of Russian folk tune.

The inspection took less than five minutes. When he was done, Pytor gestured at Gasanov with his hand, and then took a step back, waiting for his next instruction.

"Very good." Gasanov reached out to touch the bomb, running his hands along the sleek metal housing and down to the tip. He turned to his other men and dismissed them with a curt wave. They broke apart and returned to their posts.

Turning to Fish, Gasanov continued in English, "Come. Let us get a drink to celebrate," as he strode toward the room he had come from. As Fish followed, he cast a quick glance over his shoulder and noticed that the old man had returned to the bomb.

"Close the door," Gasanov said, motioning at him with a bottle of Vodka held in his left hand. Fish did as he was told, then settled in a hard plastic chair across the desk from Gasanov. Gasanov popped the top from the Vodka. *Swedish.*

He poured out two glasses and pushed one across the desk. "To the future," Gasanov said with a sly grin.

"*Salyut,*" Fish responded.

Gasanov grimaced as he took the vodka in one shot. He chased it with a second, while Fish stuck to one.

Gasanov then opened a laptop sitting on his desk and turned the screen so Fish could see it. "Now, it's time to complete this transaction."

On the screen, Fish saw the logo for the Royal Bank of Dubai. Gasanov pressed Transfer, and in a flash, fifty million Euros disappeared from his account balance.

Fish suppressed a smile. This was the second and final payment for the device. Twenty million was his. Twenty went to Jack, and the rest covered operational costs. He considered his share his severance package from the Agency.

His phone vibrated, startling him. He held up his hand, stopping Gasanov. "Just a second." He pulled out his phone and opened his email. There were three new messages. He only cared about the first. He had arranged for his bankers to send him an email when deposits over one million Euros occurred. This mail showed fifty million.

Satisfied, he closed the phone and slid it back into his pocket. "I believe our business is done then," he said, allowing a small smile.

"Yes. Yes it is," Gasanov agreed with a grin of his own. "I recommend you get as far away from this city as you can in the next day. I expect the weather conditions will become rather unfavorable." He chuckled at his own joke, then winked.

"I understand. If you need any further assistance..."

The laugh died in Gasanov's throat. His eyes narrowed. "That won't be necessary. Pytor can handle things from here. He was in the Strategic Rocket Forces, you know?"

Fish raised an eyebrow. This was news to him. "I trust you have plans for your men?" Fish added. He didn't like it that Gasanov's men had seen his face. Standard procedure would be to eliminate them.

"That is not your concern."

Fish felt his face grow hot. It was most definitely his concern. "I respectfully disagree with you on that point."

"Don't worry. I will take care of it. There will be no... how do the Americans say it? Loose strings."

Fish blinked. "Good." He would have to trust Gasanov for the moment.

"In that case..." Fish got up and turned for the door. "I have some business to attend to before I leave town."

"I'll escort you out." They walked briskly across the warehouse to Fish's car, and Fish left without another word.

As he rounded the first corner, he pulled his phone from his pocket and activated the internal encryption mechanism before punching in Jack's number.

~ * * *~

In the spot where Fish's car had been parked, Gasanov stood stock still, staring at his wrist. The second hand swept around the dial, approaching six minutes since Fish's departure.

With ten seconds left, he reached into his coat pocket and extracted a small black box with a white button on the top. He waited for the second hand to hit twelve, then he depressed the button and held his breath.

He imagined the scene: A small light would pulse underneath Fish's car. A millisecond later, an electrical charge would jump the six inches between the radio transceiver and a blasting cap stuck deep into a two-kilogram block of Semtex strapped to his axle.

The explosion would vaporize Fish, along with his car and a section of the road about three feet deep and twelve feet in diameter. A roiling cloud of smoke would be the only evidence he had ever existed.

Gasanov smiled as he felt the slight rumble reach him. He turned to Pytor. "Excellent work as usual, my old friend."

Pytor just grunted. He was neck-deep in the bomb. It was quite a bit more complex than the device he had wired to the axle of the big Mercedes.

As for the money, it was immaterial. The bomb was priceless.

Seventeen

AMANDA DROVE NORTH ON FINBOROUGH Road, hurtling along well over the speed limit. Upon reaching Redcliffe Square, she hung a hard left and pulled into a parking spot with a screech of her tires. She didn't kill the ignition. Instead, she unclipped a set of keys and handed them to Kurt.

"The blue one," she said, nodding out his window.

He was confused until he followed her gaze and realized she was talking about a townhouse. "You're not coming?"

She shook her head. "No. You'll be safe here. Make yourself at home."

"I don't know..."

"Kurt, please. I'll be back as soon as I can. Don't answer the door. Don't make any calls. In fact, give me your cell phone."

After turning over his phone, he opened the door and stepped from the car. He paused, his hand on the roof, and leaned back in. "Are you sure?"

"Yes." She looked up and down the street. "Now get inside."

He shut the door and took a step back. With a mash of gears, Amanda disappeared down the narrow street.

He shrugged and headed for the townhouse. The building was old, yet appeared well maintained, with fresh paint on the exterior and decorative landscaping in most of the small yards. A set of four narrow stairs led up to the glossy black front door.

Of the two keys Amanda had given him, only one fit the lock. He went inside and checked out the ground floor. The interior was ultra-modern, with several large windows, blond Ikea-style furniture, and tasteful decorations. Something was missing, though. Something he couldn't put his finger on... Then he realized what it was; it didn't feel as if anyone lived there. There was no mail on the counter, no dishes in the sink, no sign anyone ever used the kitchen.

Either this woman is a complete neat freak, or—I don't know, he admitted to himself. It didn't make sense. Frustrated, he made his way back to the living room and took a seat on one of the sleek leather couches bracketing a glass coffee table.

He leaned his head back, intending to get his thoughts in order, and closed his eyes.

Just a minute, He thought. *Until I figure things out.*

Then he was out.

~ * * *~

Amanda pulled into the underground garage of a squat, steel and glass building. She had to go down two levels before finding a free spot.

As she got out of the Mini, she patted her pocket,

verifying the memory card was still there. She made her way across the garage to the elevator, a small three-person affair, pressed the Up button, and waited.

It didn't take long. The doors opened with a bong, and she stepped inside. She studied the control panel. *There. A microphone. Above the buttons.* She leaned in close. "Nigel. It's Amanda."

After a brief wait, the elevator lurched into motion. Amanda felt a slight twinge of guilt at leaving Kurt behind, but she needed to move fast, and she didn't feel like answering his questions. Not yet, at least. That would come later, after she had met with Nigel.

The elevator chimed, and the doors slid open, revealing a sun-drenched room that stretched the entire length of the building. It was Amanda's first time here since Nigel Hawthorne had purchased the entire ninth floor two years earlier. "Nigel?" she called out as she stepped from the elevator.

Behind her, the doors *snicked* shut. She heard a low electric hum that appeared to be growing louder, and a moment later, Nigel Hawthorne zoomed into view from behind a rack of computer servers, his custom-built wheelchair skidding to a stop only inches from her feet.

At first glance, Nigel looked nothing like a computer hacker. He had a full head of sandy-blond hair, piercing green eyes, and an easy grin on his wide face. His arms were huge, ropy and solid. It wasn't until she looked below his waist that the picture changed. A light fleece blanket covered his withered, useless legs.

At forty-two, Nigel had been in a wheelchair for

only seven years, the result of a tragic rock climbing accident in the Pyrenees. By all rights, he should have died in the fall when he plummeted over a hundred feet after a handhold broke loose. Instead, he had spent nearly a year in the hospital recovering from a broken back, and he was now a paraplegic.

"How are you?" he asked, opening his arms for a hug.

Obliging him, Amanda leaned in for the hug, and then stepped back to take a better look at him. "You're looking good, Nigel," she said, meaning it. The last time they had met in person, he had recently completed physical therapy for his accident, and his outlook on life had been bitter.

Nigel beamed. "I just got back from a trip to the States," he said, almost unable to contain himself. "I went climbing in Utah with a group of Americans, disabled people like myself. It was fabulous!"

"Climbing? That's wonderful, Nigel!" The mountains, Amanda knew, were one of Nigel's great passions, and when the doctors had told him he would never be able to climb again, he had nearly given up on himself.

"Do you have pictures?" she asked. "I'd love to see them sometime."

Nigel nodded enthusiastically. "I sure do." His smile dimmed a bit. "But I know that's not why you're here today. What's up?" He cocked his head in anticipation.

Amanda pursed her lips. "I'd love nothing better than to talk about your trip, but I'm afraid you're right. I'm here on business."

"I knew it." He spun his chair and headed toward a sitting area outlined by three sleek, black leather couches. "Come!" he commanded, waving his hand.

Chagrined, Amanda followed him across the cavernous room. She took a seat on the closest couch while he slid his chair into a gap between the other two, a space that gave him a command view of the entire room.

"So?" he said, locking his wheels in place. "Let's hear it."

Amanda pulled the memory card from her pocket and handed it across. "I've recently come into some information—through a friend of a friend." Nigel maintained a poker face, waiting for her to provide some background.

"I've done a little bit of analysis, a cursory glance really, and it's... disturbing. It's all classified, and it's wrapped in some heavy-duty encryption. That's why I brought it to you." Nigel raised an eyebrow. The most predictable way to get him excited, she knew, was to give him a tough problem to solve. Encryption and classified data were the perfect incentive.

"British?" he asked.

She shook her head. "No. American."

He seemed lost in thought for a moment, as if considering the source. "I assume you need the information last week?"

Amanda blushed. "You assume correct. Most of the documents I examined refer to dates in the past couple of days. I've got a feeling something really big is about to go down."

She didn't want to say too much. After all, she wasn't acting as an agent of the government. At the same time, neither was he. She didn't fear he would turn around and sell the information or return it to the

CIA, but she had learned the hard way that people sometimes did strange, unexpected things.

Nigel was silent for a moment, staring down at the memory card in his hand. Then, he looked up and met Amanda's eyes. "This is personal, isn't it?"

Amanda looked away, biting back a crushing wave of despair. "Very. A good friend of mine died getting this information."

"Right. I'm sorry. Give me a minute to make a copy, and I'll take a look." He unlocked his chair and rolled out, heading toward his computer room. The only thing remaining was to negotiate a price for his services. Amanda hated that part.

Not two minutes later, Nigel rolled back into the room. He handed her the original memory card. "Copying it was no problem," he announced. "I've kicked off a stego-check, just in case." The steganographic analyzer was a computer program that looked for hidden patterns in standard data. It was just one of a whole arsenal of tools he would employ to crack the data.

"Thanks, Nigel. I really appreciate this. You have no idea."

He waved her off. "It's nothing. I've been casting around for a new challenge. Things have been slow the past few months." *He really does look good*, Amanda thought. Tanned. Rested. Almost glowing.

"I guess the last thing to discuss is—"

Nigel obviously knew where she was headed and stopped her in her tracks. "Don't worry about it. We'll work something out."

"You're a dear, Nigel," she said, standing. She gave him a quick peck on the cheek.

"Anything for you, Amanda."

"You've got my number?" He nodded.

"In that case, I should get back on the road. It's... complicated..."

"Say no more..."

"When this is over," she added. "I want us to sit down with a good bottle of wine and look at your pictures."

"You can count on it."

Eighteen

MASON CHECKED UP AND DOWN the street to verify Amanda was not circling. He counted to twenty, took a deep breath, and checked once more.

"I'll be right back," he told the taxi driver, as he stepped into the muggy afternoon heat. He looked right, left, and then dashed across the street to the building, taking care to look as if he belonged there.

While he had been waiting for Amanda to leave, he had been busy planning the next phase of the operation. As soon as he was done here, if he hadn't heard from Helen or Jack, he intended to dispose of the taxi driver and arrange for a more anonymous mode of transportation, maybe a motorcycle. He felt a small twinge of guilt at his plans for the driver. The man seemed to get quite a kick out of following Kurt and Amanda around central London. It didn't hurt that he saw Pound signs in his eyes either. If Mason were to pay him, which he had no intention of doing, his fare would be well over five hundred pounds by now. *Oh, well. He served his purpose.*

Mason reached for the door handle, but let his hand fall short as he noticed the lobby was unmanned. Instead, he straightened, pasted a surprised look on his face, and pulled his phone from his pocket. He put it up to his ear and started to speak as if he had someone on the other end.

"Hello," he mouthed. Meanwhile, his eyes were busy recording the positions of the security cameras located in the lobby. He counted three small smoked domes in the ceiling, the same kind of cameras one would find in a Las Vegas casino.

He bobbed his head, as if in an imaginary conversation. "Got it." *There may be audio surveillance, too,* he thought. "Love you, too," he said, making sure to enunciate every word in perfect British English.

Mason entered the lobby and breathed a sigh of relief as the air conditioning dried the sweat on his forehead. He strolled to a bare granite desk located beside the elevator. A building directory hung over the desk. All of the floors had names except the top, he noted. That was all he needed.

"Just drive," he told the taxi driver, as he climbed into the back seat. "I don't care where." With a tired groan, the driver shifted into gear and pulled back into the never-ending flow of traffic.

As soon as Mason felt the car pull forward, he took out his phone and typed a quick request to Helen. Architectural drawings. Blueprints. Utility information. The works.

A plan was beginning to emerge.

Nineteen

N IGEL OPENED THE REFRIGERATOR UNDER his desk
and grabbed a bottle of mineral water. He
twisted off the cap and flicked it into the
trashcan a few feet away. He turned back to his
screen.

First things first, he thought. He wanted to run
some analytical queries against Amanda's data to get a
feel for the context. His initial analysis hadn't turned
up anything of interest, but that didn't mean that
nothing was there. A full analysis would take several
hours.

He fired up several applications. The purpose of the
first program was to perform a more thorough
steganographic analysis of the unencrypted data. The
second application would execute a series of
increasingly aggressive decryption algorithms in
parallel. Since the data originated in a classified
environment, and the creators had never planned for
its release, Nigel figured he had a good chance of
cracking it. He was counting on it.

If his lightweight decryption tool wasn't able to

crack the code, it would automatically send the offending files to his server farm in the other room, where yet another set of tools would perform a more thorough, brute force decryption attack.

Once he had the software configured to his satisfaction, Nigel pressed the green button labeled Start. He took a long pull of his water. The next step was to perform some human analysis on the data, to try to get a feel for the context.

On his right was a nondescript box with four unlabeled push buttons that allowed him to switch between the American, British, and French government networks, as well as the public internet. He changed the network switch to the American setting and opened the data files.

The first subdirectory contained personnel records from an organization deep within the CIA. He scanned through the files, noting the names and the organizational structure. It looked like a man named Jack Carson was running the show. He had twenty-four direct reports, ranging from field operatives to administrative staff. Nigel sketched out the structure on a legal pad.

Next, he moved to a folder titled Games. He scanned through the contents, reading the executive summaries at the top of each document. These were war-game, far-flung scenarios created by the CIA in an effort to plan for future conflicts. The overall theme of the games revolved around removing Russia as a world player. They were recent, having all been drafted within the past five years. *Interesting.*

He moved on. The next directory contained several hundred megabytes of exported email. He double-clicked on one, and his screen filled with gibberish. *Encrypted.* He made a note.

He closed the email and clicked on another with the same result. "Damn it!" He cursed under his breath. *Why isn't this ever easy?* He made a note to come back to the folder and moved on.

Next was a series of videos. He watched a few; none were longer than a half-minute, and he quickly decided they didn't contain anything of use. The next twenty minutes was more of the same. He came across a few more encrypted files, but for the most part, they were administrative documents of little value.

Satisfied he had seen everything important, he checked the status of the decryption process. The system was busy chewing through the emails. That was encouraging. Still, there was nothing to do but wait. The progress bar at the bottom of his screen showed sixty percent. Nigel did the math in his head. That meant another hour or two before everything finished. He had some time to kill, some time to do a little digging of his own.

His fingers danced across the keyboard as he navigated to a CIA search engine, plugged in 'Jack Carson,' and hit Enter. He got no results. Scratching his chin, Nigel shifted to a different search engine and tried again. Still nothing.

He tried the next name on the list with the same result. "Hmmm." *This doesn't make sense. Either these people don't exist, or this is all an elaborate hoax.*

He had an idea. He switched the network back to the public internet and waited a moment as his computer reconfigured itself. Then he went to Google. He repeated his search, and on the fifth name, Michael

Vetter, he got a hit—an obituary listing in the online edition of the Washington Post. Nigel clicked on the link and blazed through the article, absorbing every detail. He read it twice.

Stunned, he leaned back in his chair and chewed on his lip. The obituary said Michael Vetter had died at the hands of a carjacker outside of Washington, DC. It listed his employer as the Department of Agriculture. *Yeah, right*, Nigel thought, flipping back to the personnel records.

There was no doubt. This was the same man.

He kept digging, his excitement mounting by the second.

Twenty

SOMETHING ENORMOUS BOOMED IN THE distance, right over the visible horizon. The air seemed to bristle, to pulse as if squeezed in a giant fist. The leading edge of a hazy shock wave became visible, racing towards Helen, following the curvature of the earth.

She gasped and tried to run, but her feet wouldn't move. Panicked, she looked down. *Where are my feet?*

Ropy, thorn-studded vines encased her ankles, snaking up her calves, and disappearing into the skin of her thighs. *What?* They were moving. The vines, faster now, reached for her thighs. She looked up. The hard edge of the shock wave was almost upon her. She cried out.

"Helen! Wake up, goddamn it!"

Huh? The vines withered, disintegrated and took to the wind in a fine brown dust.

Helen opened her eyes. *Jack.* He was standing over her, reaching for her shoulder.

"Jack?" She groaned, rubbing her eyes with balled fists. *My feet!* She looked down. Her feet were okay. It was just a dream.

"Good. You're awake. We've got a situation," Jack announced. "I need you at your desk." He retreated to the door.

Helen blinked and checked her watch. It was morning. Two hours ago, she had retreated to the crash tank, one of several sanctuaries scattered around the campus, built to accommodate staffers pulling long hours. The room was soundproof and featured a small single bed, a digital alarm clock, and a selection of snacks.

Jack motioned for her to hurry.

"What is it?" she asked, as she pushed herself into a sitting position.

"Those searches you set up—we've had some hits. My screen lit up like a Christmas tree about twenty minutes ago."

Helen came wide-awake at this news. The previous day, she had injected a series of small software programs into the Rapier system. The process was similar to that used by a plumber when tracing a leaky pipe. Water, or information in this case, went in one end, and the plumber, or her software tools, looked for traces throughout the system. These traces served to identify what was going on inside, along with who was using it and how.

Helen levered herself up and strode to the door. She pulled Jack down the hallway in her excitement. "That was fast! Do you have any idea who? Or where?"

"London. As for who—I've got my suspicions, but I need you to confirm them."

She realized he was holding something back. Stopping in the middle of the hall, she turned and blocked him. "Who is it, Jack? I need to know."

"Not here," he said, looking over her shoulder at a crowd of people coming their way.

She held his gaze for a moment. "Okay." She turned on her heel and continued down the hall to the secure door leading to their offices. She withdrew her badge from her pocket and pressed it up against a flat metal panel. The light turned green. She put her eye to the rubber-sheathed retina scanner, and a second light blinked green. Cleared, she leaned into the heavy door and pushed through, letting it swing shut behind her. Jack followed a moment later.

Helen raced to her computer and logged in, fumbling her password on the first try.

"Well?" Jack asked.

"Hold on." She flicked through the results, absorbing the reports as fast as she could. "Holy shit! It's Nigel. Nigel Hawthorne."

Jack gritted his teeth. "That's what I thought. Mason called while you were in the tank. I ran a check on the building he's been watching, and it turns out Nigel Hawthorne owns the entire top floor."

Helen took a deep breath, trying to control her racing pulse. "Why didn't you get me up earlier?"

"I wanted to be sure." This was a major development. If Nigel Hawthorne was involved, she had to move fast.

She focused on the screen, skipping through the evidence of Nigel's presence. "These are really specific, Jack."

"I know. He has our data."

"Uh huh. It's the only way ... Who's he working for these days?"

Jack shrugged. "Independent, last I heard."

Helen felt a growing unease with this news. She was good at her job, one of the best in the business. Nigel Hawthorne, however, was in a different league. He was a true master with deep ties to a host of intelligence services around the world. If he was working against them now, then it wouldn't be long before he figured out the whole plan.

"Shit! Shit! Shit!" she spat, the corners of her mouth turning down into a grim frown. There was only one way to fix this problem. He had to go. She would have to kill him.

The problem was that too many people would notice Nigel's death, people Helen didn't want to count as enemies. If anyone traced the hit back to Jack, or worse, to her, there would be hell to pay. The thought chilled her to her core. But, it was the only option.

"I'll take care of it," she announced.

Jack gave her a grim smile. "Burn this thing to the ground Helen. No trace."

She closed her eyes and swallowed hard. "Consider it done."

She picked up the phone, already dialing Mason's number as Jack walked away.

While she waited for the call to connect, she thought of the last time she had spoken with Nigel. It was at a conference in Atlanta six months earlier where he had presented a brilliant paper on a new variant of quantum encryption. She had bumped into him at the airport on the way home and managed to spend a half hour picking his brain while they waited for their respective flights. She pushed the thoughts aside.

"Hello?" Mason answered.

"It's me."

"What's up?" She could hear a lot of noise in the background. It sounded like a pub.

"You've got the green light."

The sound of glasses clinking and the low hum of conversation was all she could hear. Then, Mason came back, "Got it."

Helen forced her feelings about Nigel to the back of her mind, trying her best to put the mission first. She was only partly successful. "I'll send you the logistics in a few minutes." She hung up without waiting for an answer.

With a sigh, she turned back to her computer and began preparing a targeting and logistics package. She had a long day ahead of her.

Twenty-One

NIGEL RUBBED HIS TEMPLES AND squeezed his eyes shut, unable to believe what his computer was telling him. The decryption process was humming along, churning out new clear-text files every few seconds. As the files came out of his decryption program, another tool picked them up and integrated them into a cohesive picture.

He had examined several of these connections, and now wished he hadn't. They painted an undeniable picture of a complex and deadly web, originating in the CIA and stretching around the world to the Russian Federation. The planning required for such a far-reaching operation was staggering, the sort of coordinated effort he hadn't seen in years.

What really scared him was the plan itself. The CIA, using a group of Chechen rebels as a proxy, was about to start a nuclear war, a combined first-and-last strike at the heart of the Russian Federation. The data was incomplete, but this much was clear: It was real, and it was in motion.

The one thing he had not been able to confirm was

the date. However, if the financial transactions were any guide, it was soon, very soon.

Frustrated and exhausted, he pushed back from his desk and rolled down the hall toward the kitchen. On his way, he passed a series of black-and-white, high-definition security monitors displaying the streets surrounding his building. Below the monitors was an alarm console.

It was green across the board.

Twenty-Two

MASON CHECKED HIS WATCH AND smiled. He had been in the same cramped position for the past hour, reviewing floor plans and security documents, trying to find a way in. He preferred to use stealth when possible, but that was looking less likely the more he looked.

With his mouse cursor, Mason traced along the perimeter. Wherever he found a security camera, he clicked the mouse and placed a marker. The software then projected a camera coverage pattern over the virtual streetscape. He completed his circuit of the building and blew air out sharply. "Damn it!"

The combined camera coverage from the building and the ubiquitous City of London surveillance system created an impenetrable blanket. There was no way he could get in without disabling at least some of the cameras, and that would create its own problems. Alarms. Police. *No. That won't work.* He kept looking.

Realizing he was out of options, he switched from the architectural drawing to a spreadsheet containing a list of the building materials used in the refit of the top floor.

With a few clicks, Mason found what he was seeking. The windows. A smile grew on his face. "Sloppy. Very sloppy," he murmured as he congratulated himself.

The windows that covered the ninth floor were standard heavy-duty office glass. They were shatterproof and UV resistant. However, they weren't bulletproof. *It'll have to do*, he decided.

Mason closed the computer, tucked it into his bag, and turned to a long black case beside him. Inside, a Heckler & Koch PSG1 lay cradled in black rubber foam. In his line of work, Mason had exposure to a variety of exotic killing devices, but he kept coming back to this particular rifle when he had to do it from a distance. The rifle came from the same CIA safe house on the West End where he had stashed the taxi driver's body.

He assembled the rifle with practiced efficiency. Once he confirmed everything was in order, he set it aside and pulled two full magazines from the case. The first contained standard NATO 7.62x51 cartridges. The second contained a custom high-explosive round designed for penetrating armor.

With a steady hand, he unloaded both magazines and reloaded them in a new pattern. He pushed in one standard round, followed by two high-explosive rounds, repeating this pattern until the magazine was full. The first standard round was for Hawthorne. The explosive rounds would go into his computer equipment.

Satisfied with his plan and preparations, Mason inserted a magazine into the sniper rifle, chambered a round, and settled in to wait.

Twenty-Three

N IGEL RETURNED TO HIS COMPUTER as the last batch of files exited the decryption process. Like a kid on Christmas morning, he checked the results, hoping to find an answer to the riddle of when.

Bloody hell! July sixteenth? He checked his watch. *That's tomorrow!*

"Oh, Amanda. What have you gotten yourself mixed up in this time?" he whispered.

"I have to call someone," he said aloud. "But, who?" The Americans were out. So were the British. He considered the Russians for a moment, but discarded the idea. He had some contacts on the inside of the FSB, the successor to the notorious KGB, but it would take too long to cut through the bureaucracy.

Nigel drummed his fingers on the arms of his wheelchair, trying to force his tired brain to come up with a workable answer. There was only one option, he concluded. First, he had to call Amanda. She deserved to know, even though this was way over her head. Then, he had to call all of his contacts in western intelligence, as many as he could, and alert them all, scream it at the top of his lungs. The American leadership wasn't crazy enough to sanction something this monstrous. The only plausible explanation was that it was a rogue operation, something initiated by an overzealous underling. That was the only scenario that made sense.

He rolled the idea around in his head for a moment, testing the possibilities, before realizing the fatal flaw. *What if this is sanctioned at the highest level?* It was not out of the realm of possibility, he knew, for someone to have sanctioned the operation while building in enough of a buffer to escape blame if things went wrong. It had happened before.

"Shit!" He banged his fist down on the arm of chair in frustration.

First things first—he would call Amanda. He picked up the phone and punched in her number, hesitating slightly before he hit the last digit.

One ring. "Hello?"

"It's Nigel."

The phone made a bumping noise as she shifted ears. "Hold on, I need to go somewhere where I can talk." Nigel took a deep breath, trying to steady his nerves.

"I'm back. Sorry about that."

"Don't worry." He steeled himself. "We need to meet as soon as possible. The thing we discussed—"

She cut him off. "Half an hour. Your place."

"Okay. I'll shoot you a summary. It'll be there in a minute."

He dashed out a short email describing the high points of his analysis. After encrypting it with

Amanda's public key, he pressed send.

"I've got it," she announced.

"Good. I'll see you soon."

Nigel hung up the phone and sat up straight, rolling his shoulders, trying to get the kinks out. For the first time in his life, he was scared.

Twenty-Four

STRAINING TO HEAR WHAT NIGEL was saying, Mason increased the gain on his laser microphone. It was no use. He had turned away, and his voice was no longer detectable.

Nevertheless, Mason had learned something. It appeared Nigel had discovered something in the data. He had called Amanda, and she was on her way. Mason considered reporting to Helen, but decided to wait.

He had a choice to make. He could take Nigel this very moment and deal with Amanda and Vetter later, or he could be patient and get them at the same time. The complicating factor was Kurt Vetter. He hadn't shown up with the woman the last time, and there was no way to guarantee he would be here this time either. He was the wild card. Mason chewed his lip, mulling the possibilities. *Keep it simple*, he told himself. That made the decision easy. *I'll take Hawthorne now and deal with the others later.*

He shifted his eye away from the scope and blinked several times. The window in front of him was open, and the tip of his sound suppressor was flush with the edge of the glass, undetectable from the street below. Of course, once he started firing, anyone on the street who happened to look up would know exactly where it originated. This was an acceptable risk. He had taken far worse over the years.

There was movement across the street, and Mason tensed as his target rolled back into position behind his computer. He forced himself to relax. He put his eye against the scope and gave the rifle a slight nudge to the left to better center it on the man's head. His chosen trajectory had the bullet entering high on the back of Nigel's skull and exiting somewhere around his nose.

It was now or never, he decided. Mason slipped his finger into the trigger guard. He relaxed, emptying his lungs in a long, smooth exhalation. He watched Nigel for a moment longer and then, with a controlled pull, he applied an even three pounds of pressure to the trigger.

The gun coughed once, the recoil absorbed by the thick foam shoulder pad he had placed between himself and the butt. He grimaced. It all happened so fast he couldn't see the exact sequence of events.

There was a small hole in the glass across the street. Beyond the glass was a scene of absolute destruction. Nigel Hawthorne was no more. Where his head had been was nothing but a shattered pulp, like a watermelon dropped on a concrete sidewalk. *Right on target.*

Next up was an explosive round. Mason hadn't fired one of these before, and he was curious about the effect on the other end, not that he doubted it would be devastating. He shifted his aim, centering on a cluster of computer hardware stacked under the desk. He pulled the trigger, shifted, pulled, shifted, pulled. He wiped his brow and allowed himself a slight smile. Nigel Hawthorne was dead, and his apartment was in flames.

Rocking back on his haunches, Mason quickly broke down the rifle, placing each piece into its designated foam slot. He was in no hurry. The fire would serve as adequate distraction for his escape. He snapped the case shut and pulled his phone from his pocket, opened his text messaging application.

He punched in 'Phase one complete,' and sent the message.

Twenty-Five

AMANDA FIRST REALIZED SOMETHING WAS wrong when she was four blocks from Nigel's flat. A bright red fire truck blew past her, the *nee-nor, nee-nor* of the siren shredding the gentle summer evening. Right behind was a pair of ambulances, both lit up and wailing like their counterpart.

"What the—"

She looked both ways, jammed on the gas, and took off in hot pursuit, almost colliding with a third, slower ambulance as it came roaring up beside her.

She had only been back at her flat for a few minutes when Nigel's call had come in. Despite Kurt's protests, she had instructed him to stay put. She would have answers soon, she promised. Now she wondered. *Will I?*

On the bumper of the third ambulance, she rounded the corner to Nigel's block. The top floor was a raging inferno. The flames cast a jittery orange and red glow on the surrounding buildings and reflected onto the faces of the people watching from the street. Smoke billowed from broken windows, twisting and curling up into the night.

Amanda pulled over and, leaving the door ajar and the engine running, leaped from her car. A few steps ahead, the police had constructed a makeshift roadblock. She scanned the police working the roadblock, picked a young man, probably no more than twenty-five, and strode over to him.

"What's going on?" she asked, struggling to resist the urge to race into the building, to take matters into her own hands.

"Dunno, miss," he replied in a deep south-London accent. He looked over his shoulder at the fire. "I got here a few minutes ago myself." He held out his hand, palm out. "You'll have to stand back. This space is reserved for emergency vehicles."

Amanda could feel the heat from the inferno from her current position, about 300 feet away. It was like staring into an open kiln. "Do you know if anyone got out?"

"No. I don't. I'm sorry."

Amanda turned from the police officer and pulled out her mobile phone. She punched in Nigel's number. "Come on, Nigel. Pick it up," she pleaded. The heat was making her sweat. She took a few steps away.

The phone rang and rang, before finally rolling over to voice mail. She hung up and redialed. It was no use. Nigel wasn't answering.

Head down, Amanda wandered back to her car and sat on the hood. She watched the burning building and considered her options. Either Nigel was still inside, or he was somewhere in the crowd, looking for her. She had to know.

She left her car and walked along the police

cordon, putting some distance between herself and the young officer. He seemed to be the only one on this end of the street. With a furtive glance, she lifted the tape and ducked under.

Head held high and shoulders back as if she belonged there, she went to the nearest fire truck. Ducking around the side of the truck, she opened a panel and found what she was looking for—a fire jacket. She shrugged it on, then added a helmet for good measure. It would have to do. She set out to get some answers.

Ten minutes later, she had them. Nigel was not in the crowd. A police officer at the other end of the street, another young one, informed her that no one had come out of the building yet. "It's still too hot to enter," he had said, shaking his head. "A total loss. A tragedy."

Amanda returned to her car. She shed the jacket and helmet, leaving them in a neat pile at the edge of the cordon.

Why? Why Nigel? A dark thought crossed her mind. *Was it intentional?* She ruminated on it, considering the angles. Nigel was too valuable to kill. If someone had put a contract on him, then whatever he had discovered must have been huge.

As she sped toward home, her mind struggled with what to do next. If she was right and someone had killed Nigel, then she and Kurt were no doubt next on the killer's hit list. Amanda's stomach churned as she realized Nigel's killer had probably been in the crowd watching the blaze. He would have stayed, waiting to see who turned up, and she, like a good little soldier, had shown her face.

Paranoia coursed through her body. She checked her mirror. Someone was out there, hunting her, hunting Kurt. It had started with Mike, and they wouldn't stop until they had the data back.

"Damn it!" She slammed the steering wheel with her palm. "How could I have been so stupid?" She cursed herself for letting her guard down, for not trusting her instincts. When Mike Vetter was involved, things always got complicated. His brother, it seemed, carried the same curse.

Amanda checked her mirrors again. The evening traffic was thick, and anyone could be behind her, lurking in the mélange of vehicles coursing through the arteries of the city. However, she realized, she could use the traffic to her advantage. Seeing a gap ahead, she twisted the wheel hard to the left and skidded around a corner. Stomping on the gas, she wove through traffic, trying to put as much distance between herself and her imagined tail as possible.

Her breathing came a little easier after making a few random turns, a few stops and starts. Maybe there was no tail after all? Kurt. She had to get back. They would be coming for him, for her. *They may already be there.* She had to warn him.

She grabbed her phone and thumbed through to her home number. "Come on, Kurt, pick up!" It rang four times and then went silent. She tried again with the same result.

"Damn it!"

She dropped the phone into the center console and returned her focus to the road. Images of Kurt, dead on her couch, flashed through her mind, making her press harder and harder on the accelerator. If she went any faster, she was liable to cause an accident, or worse, attract the attention of the police, something she could ill afford.

Ten minutes later, she pulled onto her street a little over a block from her house. She slowed the car and scanned for anything out of the ordinary. A pair of young women jogged by, smiling at her as they passed. They continued past her house and disappeared around the next corner. Satisfied there was nothing out of order, Amanda goosed the throttle and zoomed into her spot.

With a final check, she climbed from the car and, keys in hand, dashed up the stairs. The front door was secure, as she had left it, and when she crashed through, Kurt looked up, startled. She locked the door behind her.

"Hey," he said, startled. Then he noticed her expression, stood and came over to her. "What is it?"

Amanda choked back a sob. *Nigel.* She would grieve later. She gave Kurt the condensed version, finishing with her theory of the next target.

"You're sure?" he asked.

"As much as I can be." She turned and headed up the stairs, taking them two at a time.

"Wait! Where are you going?" Kurt called from the landing.

"Wait there. I'll be right back."

She turned into the first room at the top of the stairs and crossed to a stack of still-packed moving boxes lining the far wall. Scooting one aside, she dropped to her knees and pressed her palm against the wainscoting nearest the window.

The panel gave a soft *click* and popped open,

revealing a hidden wall safe. Amanda entered her combination, and the lock disengaged. She extracted a black backpack from within. Kurt appeared behind her.

Amanda frowned at him "I thought I told you to wait downstairs."

"What's that?" Kurt said, motioning at the pack.

"Money and guns," she said, getting to her feet. "Is your stuff packed?" Kurt rolled his eyes. "I never unpacked."

"Good. Let's go."

"Hold on." Kurt went to the window and peered out. "I don't see anything."

Amanda turned and, leaving him alone by the window, she dashed down the stairs. She waited for him in the foyer, turning to face him as he caught up with her. "Listen very closely. I believe the same people that killed your brother killed my friend. The only thing in common is that memory card. They're coming for us next."

A flash of fear crossed his face. "Okay. What next?" he asked.

"I don't know," Amanda snapped. "I'll figure that out on the road."

"Okay." Kurt reached out and started to unlock the door.

Amanda grabbed his hand before he got the deadbolt open. "Careful!" She took his place, opened the door a few inches, and peered out. "We're clear."

In a blur, she yanked the door the rest of the way open and stepped onto the porch.

They dashed out to the car together and jumped in.

"Do me a favor," she asked, as they pulled out of

the parking place. "Check my email. Nigel said he was going to send me a summary."

Kurt took her phone. Out of the corner of her eye, she saw him pushing and swiping at it with his fingers, so she barked out instructions on how to open the email client. He sat hunched over the email, scrolling with his thumb, apparently reading the summary.

"What is it? What did he say," she asked, dying to know.

"Go!" Kurt replied without looking up. "Just go."

Twenty-Six

KURT'S HANDS WERE TREMBLING BY the time he finished reading the email.

"Well?" Amanda asked with an annoyed glance. Before he could answer, Amanda jerked the car to the right to dodge a wandering minivan. She leaned on the horn and shot the errant driver a vicious glare.

"What did it say?" She was breathing hard, probably from the adrenaline of the narrow escape amplifying her impatience.

Kurt took a deep breath. "In about 24 hours," he said, checking his watch, "a group of Chechens is going to detonate a nuke in downtown Moscow."

"Say again? A nuke?"

"Uh huh. It says they're using a hundred-fifty-kiloton warhead, left over from the Soviet days. But that's not all..."

Her left eyebrow arched. "What do you mean?"

"The bomb is set to go off tomorrow night. Everyone, the entire government, the military, will be in town."

"A decapitation strike," Amanda breathed. "That's

insane!"

Kurt shrugged. "This whole thing is insane. It says the bomb is located in a warehouse, downtown."

"Do we have a street address?" Amanda asked.

"We do. We even have a map."

Amanda whistled. "This is crazy, Kurt."

He shrugged and dropped the phone in the center console. Amanda plucked it out, extracted the memory card containing Mike's data, rolled down her window, and tossed the phone into the night. "Get rid of your phone, Kurt. It's not safe anymore."

They drove on for a minute, digesting the news. Amanda broke the silence first. "We need to go to Paris." She flicked the turn signal and changed lanes to catch the next exit.

Kurt was surprised. "Paris? What's in Paris?"

"A friend. Someone we can trust. If this is real, and your government—"

"It's your government, too," Kurt shot back. "And anyway, I get the impression—"

"Hold on a second," Amanda interrupted, locking eyes with him and ignoring the road. "It's a long story, and I'll spare you the details, but I am *not* a US citizen. I may work for them occasionally, but only when our goals align."

Kurt was confused. "But, I assumed..."

"You assumed wrong. That's the first rule in this business. Don't ever forget it."

Kurt chewed on that for a second. "Do you think this is real?"

"Maybe. Probably. Enough people have died to make me believe there's something behind it." Amanda left the motorway and followed the signs for the M20

South.

"So, back to your contact in Paris," Kurt said. "Why don't we go to the US Embassy in London, or take it straight to British intelligence?"

Amanda glared at him. "I thought you said you were on the inside before? You know how they work."

"Yeah. Good point... They're pretty close aren't they?" He fiddled with the window control, something to keep his hand occupied while he thought.

"So this friend in Paris, is he French intelligence?"

"She. No. American."

"Who does she work for?" he asked.

Amanda didn't answer, just kept her eyes on the road.

"So you want to take this back to the CIA? I thought you didn't trust them."

"I didn't say she's CIA. All I can tell you is that I trust her, and she has enough contacts to ferret out whether this is real."

"Are you sure she's the only one we can trust?"

"Uh huh. She's our only choice." They passed a sign indicating forty miles to the channel tunnel.

"The tunnel?" Kurt asked, incredulous.

"Yep. We should be there in less than an hour. They won't expect it."

Kurt knotted his fingers and cracked his knuckles, burning off nervous energy as he digested the news.

"Look in the top of my bag," Amanda said. "Please."

Reaching between his legs, he unzipped the top of the bag and peered inside—cash, passports, and three smart phones of the same model Amanda had tossed out the window. There were also two guns, a pair of semi-automatic SIG Sauer P220s.

He looked up at Amanda in surprise. When she didn't turn, he pulled one of the guns from the bag, making sure to keep the muzzle pointed at the floor. He pulled the slide back and looked in the chamber of each pistol. They were both loaded. He placed the guns on the floor and dug around in the bag again, straining against his seat belt.

"I know I've said this before, but you really remind me of your brother," she said quietly.

Kurt replaced the guns and met her eyes. "Really?"

"Yes. You have the same mannerisms when you work the weapon. It's eerie."

Kurt looked out the window, watching the countryside pass by on their left. "I can't believe he was involved in this."

"Me either," Amanda added, shaking her head.

"When was the last time you saw him?" he asked.

"It was in Khartoum, three years ago. I was working with MI-6..."

"So you *are* British intelligence?"

"Will you let me finish?" she said with a hint of exasperation.

"Sorry." He motioned for her to continue.

"Anyway, your brother came into the operation—this big, strapping American. He knew all the players, knew how things worked. We were running our operation under the cover of an international non-governmental organization, and things were a mess. Mike pulled it all together and got the intelligence we needed. At the same time, he drove all of the women on site crazy. He was such a charmer, you know?"

Kurt smiled, recalling the way Mike used to fill up a room with his presence.

"So, your brother and I spent a lot of time together on this mission. One night, we had a meet set up with the head of a local terror cell; a man who I can thankfully say is now dead. Things went wrong—more wrong than I've ever seen. Nevertheless, your brother, he kept his shit together. If it wasn't for him, I wouldn't be sitting here telling you this."

"What did he do?"

She sniffled, wiping a tear from her eye. "He took a bullet for me. We hadn't done our homework on the cell. Well, not we, but the people putting the mission together. A member of the cell worked in our offices, passing information back. We never stood a chance."

"That's bullshit."

"Exactly. One day I was out for my morning run with your brother, when a car pulled up and a group of men snatched us. Through the mole, they had identified him as our leader. I was an added bonus. They were going to kill us both, but not before they toyed with MI-Six.

"Shit."

She bit her lip. "It wasn't pretty. Word of our abduction got back quickly, and they put together a team to rescue us. Seven men died in the raid. By the time they got through the perimeter defenses, Mike had broken through his restraints and was working on freeing me. To make a long story short, one of the bad guys came back to check on us. When he saw we were loose, he went ape-shit and decided to finish us off right there. For some reason I still can't figure out, he went for me first. Maybe he thought shooting a woman was more sporting. I'll never know."

"Go on," Kurt said with a soft smile.

"I thought I was dead, but the bullet never came. There was a bright flash, and then your brother was on the floor bleeding like crazy from his shoulder. I think the shooter was as shocked as I was." She chuckled. "I took advantage of his confusion and jumped on him and snapped his neck like a twig." She made a twisting motion with her hands to illustrate.

"Wow." Kurt didn't know what to say.

"Your brother was fine, but taking a bullet for me was never part of the deal. I owed him my life after that. It was that simple. We got together several times over the years, for dinner, when we were in the same city, but it had been a few months since we last spoke."

"Thanks," Kurt said. "I mean it. I really appreciate hearing about that side of him."

"I know it sounds corny," she said, "but he was one of the good guys."

"This sucks."

Amanda shrugged. "It happens. Sometimes, in our line of work, the lines get a little blurry." She took Kurt's hand and squeezed it. He squeezed back. They drove in silence for a few minutes, reflecting on their loss, next steps put on hold for the moment.

Eventually, Kurt motioned toward the guns and said, "How are you going to get those across the border?"

"Don't worry about that."

"Are you sure?"

"It's not a problem. I have my ways. And a woman's got to have her secrets, doesn't she?" She grinned.

Kurt laughed, feeling a bit more relaxed with the discussion shifted away from Mike. "Okay."

Twenty-Seven

AMANDA'S HOUSE WAS EMPTY WHEN Mason arrived. However, he detected recent activity—a dirty plate in the sink, an open box of cereal on the counter. Little things.

He did a quick sweep of the ground floor and finding nothing, moved upstairs. He couldn't help but notice how empty the house felt, like a hotel. Standing in the middle of the master bedroom, he let his eyes wander, trying to put himself inside Amanda's head.

The black lacquered dresser against the far wall looked promising. So did the closet. He chose the closet first. Pockets. Shoes. Boots. Jackets. He checked them all, but came up empty. Then he turned to the shelves, climbing up on a small stool so he could get a clear view. No dice. Undeterred, Mason moved on to the next room, and then the next. He was running out of time. He had to find something, and he had to find it fast.

Finally, in the last room, he hit pay dirt. A compact wall safe was disguised behind a pop-out panel left slightly ajar. The safe was roughly eight-by-eight inches and made of brushed stainless steel. It had a kinetic dial-combination as well as a numeric key pad.

Time to call Helen.

"I need your help," he said when she answered.

"Shoot," she replied.

"I found a wall safe in the woman's flat. I need some help opening it."

Keys clicked on the other end. "Is there a model number on the door?" Helen asked.

Mason got on his knees and bent in close to read the black label affixed to the top edge. "Dyna-Safe, model tee, one, five, five, bee."

More key clattering. "It's your lucky day. Does it have a keypad?"

"It does." He resisted the urge to punch in keys at random.

"Try two, sixteen, thirty, and then enter eight, four, two, three, four."

"Wait." Mason spun the dial in the order she had dictated. "What was that number again?"

"Eight, four, two, three, four."

He punched in the numbers, and the light on the front of the safe blinked green twice, a soft 'clunk' emanated from within. *God bless the NSA,* Mason thought. Without them, he would have had to open the safe the old-fashioned way.

He pulled the door open and cursed. Empty. "Nothing here," he reported. He shut the safe, and the light changed from green to red as it rearmed.

"It was worth a try," Helen commiserated.

Mason wasn't listening. *There has to be something here.* He cast his eyes around, looking for something else, anything, that would give him a clue as to who this woman was and how she was involved.

"This is odd..." Helen said, her words trailing off.

"What is it?"

Furious typing echoed through the phone. "Their phones have stopped tracking."

"That's not so odd." He took a seat on the floor with his back against a box.

"It is when they go from seventy miles per hour to zero in less than a second." Now she had his full attention. Only two events could cause that type of behavior. Either Vetter and the woman had gotten into a horrendous crash, or they had ditched their mobile phones. *Probably the latter.*

"Uh, I think we have a problem here." He got to his feet and gazed out the window, thinking hard. "They're going to ground. Where were they headed when the beacon went dark?" he asked.

"I thought you were tracking them, too?" She sounded angry.

"I've been screwing around with this damn safe, Helen. Just answer the question!"

"Southeast."

"What's in that direction?" He had a vague mental map of the United Kingdom, but once he got a few dozen miles outside of London, things got fuzzy.

Helen didn't answer right away; instead he heard her banging away on her keyboard. "A bunch of small cities and towns, ports, an airport or two. You name it."

Mason rubbed his chin, thinking *what would I do in their situation?* He would bolt, he decided, put some distance between himself and whoever was hunting him.

"They're leaving the country." He was sure of it.

"Well, they're not flying. I sent their description out to the French police—wanted for questioning in a terrorism investigation."

"Good. Good thinking."

"That leaves two routes: The channel tunnel and the ferry system."

Mason shook his head. "The tunnel would be stupid. My money's on a ferry. Less security. Less chance of a choke-point."

She coughed. "I agree. But—what if that's what they want us to think?"

"Shit." Mason kicked one of the boxes. "It looks like I'm going to France."

"Yes, it does." She chuckled. "Weren't you complaining only a few weeks ago that you missed the field?"

He had been, and he regretted every word. "That's the last time I do that."

"Get your ass to France, Mason. I'll let you know when they pop back up. They can't stay off the grid for long."

"Okay. Later."

"Later."

Before leaving, Mason had one more thing he wanted to do. He strolled back into Amanda's bedroom, going straight for the dresser. He pulled open the bottom drawer, gazed down at the collection of lingerie neatly arrayed in front of him, and smiled. With care, he selected a pair of black lace panties, brought them to his nose, and inhaled deeply. They were clean, yet musky like a woman. He rubbed them across his cheek, relishing the sensation as the silk caught on his stubble, imagining the woman in the photo Helen had sent him peeling this same pair of lingerie from her body and offering herself to him.

That wouldn't happen, not in a million years. Still, the idea was intoxicating. He stuffed the panties in his pocket. *For later.*

Closing the drawer, Mason turned and performed one more quick survey of the room. He saw nothing else he could use in his pursuit, so he turned and headed for his car.

He grabbed the map he had purchased three hours earlier from the front seat. With his right index finger, he traced a path from his current location in downtown London back to Heathrow Airport and committed the route to memory. With luck, he would be in Paris in a couple of hours.

With a resigned sigh, he started the car and pointed it west.

Twenty-Eight

"W ATER?" AMANDA OFFERED, REACHING PAST Kurt into the back seat.

He was parched. "Sure." She handed him a half-liter bottle of Evian and kept one for herself. He cracked the top and took a long pull, draining it half-empty.

"Thanks. I needed that," he said, wiping his mouth. He screwed the cap back on and stuffed the bottle between his thighs. He yawned. On any other day, the soft *click-clack* sound of the train would have lulled him to sleep, but not today. Sleep was the last thing on his mind. "So what next?" he asked.

Boarding the train had proven to be no problem. Amanda had slipped the boarding agent an extra hundred Euro note, and he had waved them to the front of the line. It was a little disconcerting that the official was so easily bribed, but given their circumstances, he was grateful, both for Amanda's resourcefulness and for the agent's greed.

"The CIA has been one step ahead of us the whole time. Getting rid of our phones was a good first step, but we need to do more, go deeper underground."

"Okay." He wasn't sure where she was going with this.

"I'm sure our phones were monitored.

"But I had a UK SIM card..."

"It doesn't matter. You said your name when you called me. The computers probably picked it up and made the link."

He took a drink. "Can they really do that?"

Mid-sip, Amanda snorted, spraying water onto the steering wheel. "Are you kidding? Everything you say on the phone is recorded and analyzed. It's only a matter of how fast they can process the data."

"I didn't think..." When she frowned, he said, "Sorry. Go ahead."

"Just trust me on this one."

Deciding silence was best, he simply nodded.

"The bottom line is, I think we need to ditch this car and find another way to Paris. I have no doubt these guys have hooks into the international transport network, including the one we registered with when we got on the auto transport." She motioned forward, toward France. "There's a good chance there will be someone waiting on the other end."

"Damn! I didn't even consider that." Kurt had a mental image of an anonymous man putting a gun to his head and pulling the trigger. He shivered at the thought.

"I want to switch cars. Worst case, there's someone waiting for us, and it's all over. Best case, we slip through and get some distance between us before they realize we're gone. Still, once they find my car on the French side of the channel, they're going to have a pretty good idea where we're headed.

Kurt unlatched his seat belt and stretched. "That's a good idea." He hesitated. "There's one problem, though; I have no idea how to steal a car."

Amanda smiled. "It's funny..."

"What?"

"In some ways you remind me so much of your brother, but at other times, you're the complete opposite."

Kurt was annoyed at the comparison. He had been compared to Mike his whole life. For most of his teens, he had tried, without success, to be better that his brother at something, anything, but it had all been in vain. "Yeah. I get that sometimes," he said, unable to keep the trace of bitterness from lacing his voice.

"Sorry for the comparison. I know you don't want to hear it."

Kurt smiled. "Don't worry about it. It's only natural given your history."

"Anyway, don't worry about the car. I saw one on the way in." She pulled her door latch and climbed from the Mini. Kurt popped his own door and started to follow.

"Can you grab my bag?" she asked.

"Sure." He grabbed it from the front floor. He also grabbed two more bottles of water from the back seat.

"We might need it," he said.

Amanda tossed her keys onto the floor of the Mini and closed the door with a thunk. She turned and worked her way forward along the swaying railroad car. Kurt scooted around the hood and fell in behind her. "You're leaving your keys?"

She looked back and shrugged. "We don't need

them anymore."

They reached a set of stairs leading down. Amanda went first. The next level was packed, with cars arranged bumper to bumper as far as he could see. Amanda stopped beside a white Renault hatchback.

"Is this it?" he asked.

"It is." She peeled a paper tag from under the right windshield wiper.

"Where are the owners?"

She gave him a devious grin. "This car is being transported without its owner. The tag tells the people on the French end what to do with it until it's retrieved. Pickup isn't scheduled for another two days." He got it.

"Get in," she said, heading to the other side of the car. Before getting in, he noted it was a left-handed-drive vehicle, unlike Amanda's Mini. He scooted around and squeezed himself into the passenger seat.

Amanda handed him the tag from the windshield. "Put this in the glove box." She pulled the sun visor down and a pair of keys dropped into her lap.

"We should reach the end in a few minutes. When we get there, we drive off the train and go on our way. There are cameras, though, so try to keep your head down until we get out of the arrival area. In addition, we'll have to go through customs. I have another passport." She took a deep breath. "I want you to play sick, like you're passed out cold. If that doesn't work..."

"I understand." He felt stupid, like an amateur, for not having an alternate passport of his own, but he had never envisioned where the memory card from his dead brother would lead.

They only had one choice now; move forward or die.

Kurt felt the train slowing. The brakes squealed, a sharp screech echoing up and down the tunnel. A voice came on the public address system. He rolled down the window to hear it better. "We are arriving in Calais. Please prepare your belongings." Then, it repeated in French *"Nous sommes arrivers en Calais. Preparez-vous votre choses pour disembarquement."*

"This is it," Amanda said. "We're almost there." Kurt noticed her knuckles were white on the wheel. His gut clenched as he considered the implications of what they were about to attempt. He took a deep breath and steadied himself. The train rumbled and clacked to a stop. A minute later, sunlight flooded the car, nearly blinding them. They sat in silence for a few minutes as the cars in front of them disembarked. Finally, it was their turn.

Amanda turned the key, and the little diesel engine groaned to life. She inched forward until they reached the mouth of the train, where they drove out onto a ramp. Once off the train, they drove across a large parking lot toward Customs.

"Time to put on a show," she whispered as they approached the kiosk.

Kurt complied, reclining the seat and closing his eyes. He lolled his head against the passenger window and let a thin line of drool escape his mouth for added effect.

The car came to a stop and Amanda rolled her window down.

"Bonjour madam," he heard a young woman say. *"Bienvenue a la France. Passeporte s'il vous plait?"*

"Bonjour." She passed her papers through the

window.

"*Passeporte de votre mari?*" He mentally translated, "Your husband's passport?"

"*Il est tres mal au estomache. La cuisine des British est merde. S'il vous plait. Lui non a dormir depuis deux jours.*" Kurt knew enough French to understand Amanda was telling the woman he was sick to his stomach, that he hadn't eaten in several days.

The immigration official hesitated for an agonizing moment, and then relented. "Bon voyage."

Amanda rolled up the window and put the car back into gear. A few moments later, they were on the highway, heading south. Kurt opened his eyes and wiped the drool from his mouth.

"You were great!" Amanda exclaimed, touching him on the knee. An unexpected chill shot up his spine. Her hand lingered for a moment before she removed it, forcing a nervous cough.

Kurt felt a twinge of guilt, as he thought of Amelia. What would she say? He suppressed the thought, reminding himself of the women in South America. All notions of faithfulness to his dead wife had been discarded months ago.

But this was different. There was something about Amanda, something he couldn't put his finger on. She intrigued him, excited him in a way no woman had since Amelia.

"I can play sick with the best of them," he said with a sly grin.

She laughed and pressed down on the accelerator.

They were going to Paris.

Twenty-Nine

AGIANT GRIN BLOSSOMED ON Helen's face as she scanned her most recent email, received moments earlier. It was an automated message from the Rapier system:

```
2012 Mini Cooper
Color: Green
Country of Origin: UK
Registered Owner: Amanda Carter
Location: Calais, France
```

She picked up her phone and dialed Jack. No answer. She left a brief message. "They're in France."

She called Mason, getting him on the fourth ring. "Yeah?"

"We were wrong. They took the tunnel after all."

"No shit?"

"Yep. Their car was on the train in Calais. My gut tells me they took another car from the train."

"What if it's a decoy?" he asked, playing the devil's advocate.

Helen considered the possibility, but discounted it right away. Kurt and Amanda were on the run; decoys were a luxury they couldn't afford. "Unlikely. We have to assume they know the timeline by now. They're moving fast and light. Why they're in France, I have no idea. Yet. But it's the only possibility."

"Have you told Jack?"

"I left him a message. I'm heading to his office after I get off the phone with you."

Mason went silent for a moment. Helen heard a public address system in the background, loud and full of static.

"Okay. I can be in France in two hours. Where am I headed?"

She pulled up a map and ran her finger along the road south from Calais. "Paris is my bet. They must know someone there." She detected a presence behind her and glanced over her shoulder. *Jack.*

"Hold on Mason. Jack's here." She put her hand over the phone.

"You found them?" Jack asked.

"French immigration discovered the woman's car on the Eurotunnel train about an hour ago."

"Good work. Is Mason on the way?"

"I've got him on the phone right now."

"Let me have it." She handed over the phone to him.

"What's your ETA?" Jack asked.

"About two hours."

Jack chewed on this for a moment. "I may be able to call in some favors, bring in some additional muscle in Paris. I'll make some calls."

"Thanks."

"And Mason..."

"Yeah, Jack?"

"Finish this. We're out of time."

"Understood."

Jack handed the phone back to Helen. "Let me know as soon as you hear anything. Anything at all." He turned and left.

"That was odd," Mason said. "It's almost as if he isn't too concerned, or he's preoccupied or something."

Helen had noticed it, too. Considering their timeline and the threat posed by the missing information, she figured Jack would be bouncing off the walls by now. "There's so much going on..." She drummed her fingers on her keyboard, puzzling over her boss's behavior. "We can't worry about him right now. We have to trust he has his shit together. All we can do is our jobs."

"I guess so." Mason didn't sound convinced.

"Anyway, let me know as soon as you get to Paris. I'll keep digging, looking for hits on this end. I'll call you when I find out who Jack is activating."

"Okay. How about the timeline?" Mason asked. "Is everything still on track?"

Helen shrugged mentally. "As far as I can tell." She yawned. "Well, that's all I've got for now."

"Talk to you soon then." Mason ended the call.

As soon as her phone was back in the cradle, Helen got up and headed for the break room. *Coffee. I need coffee.*

Thirty

"**H**ELEN!" JACK BELLOWED FROM SOMEWHERE down the hall. Helen took a step back from the coffee machine so she could see through the break room doorway. *What the hell?* Jack was barreling down the hallway like a freight train, heading straight for the break room; and he looked pissed. *Oh shit.*

She left her coffee brewing on the machine and stepped out to meet him. "What's going on?" she asked.

"My office. Now." He turned on his heel and stormed off. Helen scrambled to catch up. *What is it this time?*

Her mind raced through the possibilities as she tried to determine if he was pissed at something she had done, something she had missed. Not ten minutes earlier, he had seemed almost lackadaisical about the status of the operation.

"Close the door," he said as they swept into his office.

Helen stopped short. "What happened here?" she

asked, nodding at the remains of a picture frame scattered across the floor. Then she noticed his secure phone, the torn cord pointing toward his chair.

Oh, wow. She had seen Jack lose his temper before, but never like this. Never violent.

He noticed the look on her face. "Don't mind that," he said, dismissing the carnage with a wave of his hand.

Helen shrugged and forced her attention back to him. He picked up a half-full glass of scotch from his desk and drained it one gulp, then walked over to the credenza and grabbed a bottle and another glass. He refilled his glass and poured one for Helen, pushing it across his desk to her.

"Fucking Chechens," he hissed, falling into his seat. *Ah. Fish.* Helen took a tentative sip of the scotch. *Good stuff,* she noted. She waited for Jack to elaborate.

"Something's up with Fish," he said after another long gulp. "He's not responding."

He turned his monitor so Helen could see. Fish's locator beacon was red, meaning he was off line. Helen didn't have access to Fish's location from her computer. Only Jack, and at one point, Mike Vetter, were allowed to see each other's movements. *Typical need-to-know bullshit.*

"Have you tried calling him?" she asked, regretting the words as soon as they left her mouth.

Jack shot her a withering glare. "What do you think?"

That was all the answer she needed. She sipped her scotch while trying to figure out what Jack was going to say next. "Damn." That was all that came to her. Since the beginning of the operation, what Fish had been doing, where he had been stationed, and who he had been working with had been above her pay grade. That Jack was coming to her now, when things were falling apart, was bullshit. She took a deep breath, steeling herself for battle.

"That's all you can say? Damn? What the fuck, Helen?" Jack blurted, spittle flying from his lips in great, boozy globs.

His ferocity surprised her, and she leaned back to put some more space between them. "I'm not sure what else to say, Jack. You've kept me in the dark about what Fish has been doing since day one. What do you expect?"

This seemed to incite him further. He banged his fist on his desk. "I don't give a shit! I need ideas, and I need them now!"

"Do we have anyone else nearby? Someone who can do a visual?"

He shook his head, swirled his scotch, and appeared to be trying to regain control of himself.

What a cluster fuck, she thought. *Sending Fish in alone...* "I don't know Jack." She put her unfinished drink on the edge of his desk. "I think we need to give it some time. This is Fish, remember. He's clever." *That sounds lame*, Helen thought.

Jack bolted to his feet and began pacing the room. "We don't have any damn time! This operation is set to go live in less than twenty-four hours!"

"Yeah. But what choice do we have?" She had him. Jack stared out the window, and Helen saw his shoulders sag. For the first time, he looked like an old, worn out man.

"I need to make a few calls," Jack said, moving toward his unsecured phone.

She waited for a moment, in case he had something else. Then, "Okay."

She got up and left before he flew off the handle again.

Thirty-One

"**W**E NEED FUEL," AMANDA ANNOUNCED unexpectedly.

Kurt leaned over and glanced at the instrument cluster. Sure enough, the gauge was sitting on empty. He looked up and pointed. "Take the next exit. There's an airport, Le Bourget. There'll be a gas station there."

Amanda switched lanes, preparing to exit the highway. The little Renault had only had an eighth of a tank of diesel when she had boosted it, barely enough to get to Paris, and not nearly enough if they ran into trouble.

"I'll pump," he volunteered as they rolled to a stop.

"Thanks. I'll be right back." She climbed out and dashed towards the restrooms.

As Kurt was screwing the gas cap back on, she returned with a coffee in one hand and a long, skinny baguette in the other. A sliver of paper-thin ham dangled from the end of the sandwich where she had already taken a bite.

"All yours," she said through a mouthful. "Good

sandwiches inside."

Kurt's stomach rumbled. It had been too long since his last meal.

"Could I get a few Euros?" he asked. He had spent the last of his supply on the fuel, feeding it bill by bill into the automated pump.

She dug into her pocket and handed him a colorful fistful of Euros. "That should cover you."

Kurt did a quick count. *More than enough.* "I'll be back in a few." He headed straight for the restrooms. Once inside, with the door locked, he turned on the cold tap and let it run. As soon as he was satisfied with the temperature, he cupped his hands under the stream and splashed his face. He did this several times, trying his best to wash away the fatigue. Face dripping, he took a handful of paper towels and cleaned himself, slicking his hair back and scrubbing his teeth with his finger. His mouth tasted like the floor of a subway.

His next stop was the store. He grabbed a large cappuccino, some gum, and a sandwich identical to Amanda's. The total came to thirteen Euros. He gave the cashier a twenty, got his change, and headed back to the car.

Amanda was on the phone speaking in a rapid-fire mixture of French and English. She gave him a look that said *hold on,* and turned away. *Must be her contact in Paris,* Kurt assumed. He leaned against the front of the car as he waited, taking small sips from his steaming coffee.

Amanda finished her call and turned to meet his eyes. "Sorry. That took a lot longer than I thought it would."

"Did you get it all straightened out?" he asked.

"I think so. She's inside the embassy. We're about thirty minutes away if traffic works in our favor. But she said we should hold off for at least an hour and a half."

"Why?"

"There's a strike going on and the streets are a mess. It's supposed to be over soon, though."

Strikes were a fact of life in the city of lights. "Okay. So we're going straight to the embassy then?" he asked with an inquisitive smile.

"Uh huh." She climbed behind the wheel and started the car. Kurt hopped into the passenger seat.

With a full tank and an hour to kill before they made their run to safety, they decided to find an internet connection and see if they could discover anything new about the people hunting them.

~ * * *~

As they pulled out of the gas station, Amanda thought of her contact in the embassy. Liza Barnett was one of her oldest friends, going back all the way to her college days at Stanford. They had been roommates their first year of school, striking up an immediate and deep friendship within their first months of university. Liza had taken a job with the Department of State eight years ago, working her way up to her dream posting in Paris. Amanda's life had taken a different trajectory, but they had managed to stay in touch despite the differences in their lifestyles.

Liza was the Deputy Chief of Mission, and she wielded enormous influence over day-to-day operations, running the less-public side of the American mission in France. If there was anyone Amanda trusted in Europe, it was Liza.

Coming up on their right was a row of hotels. "Keep your eyes open," she told Kurt. "Look for a Wi-Fi sign."

"Uh huh."

"How about that one?" she asked, tapping the brakes and pointing at a well-lit hotel on their right.

"I guess." Kurt shrugged.

Thirty-Two

L IZA BARNETT RUBBED HER HANDS together under the roaring dryer and watched as the last beads of water raced away from the blast of hot air. Finished, she checked her watch. She had a little over an hour until Amanda arrived. And still, she couldn't stop replaying the strange conversation in her head.

"Hello? This is Liza Barnett," she had said upon answering her mobile phone. A United Kingdom number had displayed on the caller ID.

"Liza. Don't say my name. Do you have a minute?"

It's Amanda, she realized.

"Sure." Her morning had been off to a slow start since her boss was in Brussels. Paperwork, personnel issues, busy work.

"I need your help with something this morning. It's time sensitive."

"Okay," she replied without hesitation. "Tell me."

A pause. "I can't give you details over the phone."

Liza cocked her head, intrigued. "Are you in trouble?"

Silence again. Then, "We're on our way in. We may

be coming in hot."

Amanda felt a flush of excitement. *Coming in hot?* "We? And what do you mean by coming in hot?"

"I'm not alone." She heard a male voice in the background.

"Who are you with?"

"A friend. That's all I can say." She sounds serious, Liza decided. Besides, Amanda would never joke about something like this.

I'll have to contact security, she thought, *to clear the way.* Like all US embassies around the world, security had been enhanced after 9/11 to prevent all manner of attacks on the embassy itself, with heavy concrete barriers, a dense maze of crowd-control gates, and a host of other less-visible security measures put in place to control access. A detachment of U.S. Marines with orders to kill guarded the gate.

"How hot exactly?" Her imagination was running wild.

"Take your worst case and double it."

Liza froze, gripping the phone so hard her knuckles turned white. "Do you have any idea what you're asking for?"

"I do."

She grabbed a pen and a pad of paper. "What are you driving?" They passed the next few minutes exchanging details on the vehicle Amanda would be arriving in and the most direct route through the city. Liza briefed Amanda on the current transit strike, giving her tips on how to avoid the disrupted areas. Once these arrangements were complete, Liza tried to push the conversation back to the personal level, to get a feel for how much trouble her friend was really in.

Amanda resisted, telling her they would catch up when the dust settled. She gave up. She had preparations to make, wheels to set in motion. She moved to end the call.

"Be careful," she intoned.

"I will."

She terminated the connection and sprang into action.

Thirty-Three

W ITH A HARSH RING, HELEN'S secure phone destroyed her train of thought. She checked the caller ID. NSA.

"Bartholomew here."

"Helen, this is Patrick. I've got a hit on that name you gave me." Helen sat up straighter. Patrick Morrison was a former CIA colleague who had transferred to the NSA two years earlier. An hour ago, on a hunch, she had called him and asked for a favor.

"A strange call came into the embassy in Paris six minutes ago. The caller, a woman, didn't identify herself, but the receiver did."

"Who was it?"

She heard papers shuffling. "Liza Barnett. It says here she's the Deputy Chief. I ran her through the system, and it looks like she was roommates with the woman you're been looking for, at Stanford."

"You're a dear, Patrick," she gushed, a shit-eating grin spreading across her face.

"Just doing my job," he replied with mock modesty. "And get this. The caller is coming into the embassy within the next hour. She asked the deputy for a welcoming party, said something about 'coming in hot.' I'm guessing you're the one applying the heat?"

Avoiding his question, Helen asked one of her own. "What do you mean 'a welcoming party'?"

She heard keys tapping, then he said, "The transcription is on the way."

Her computer beeped, and she saw an email from Patrick sitting at the top of her inbox. She opened and scanned it. "Shit," she said under her breath.

"I'm not sure what you want to do with this, Helen," Patrick said, getting serious again. "We're talking about the deputy ambassador here. There are some pretty serious political ramifications if you fuck with someone like that."

She was done talking. "I've got to go now, Patrick." She terminated the call before he could respond.

She forwarded the email to Jack. It didn't solve the problem with Fish and the Chechens, but it could signal a quick end to their data problem. If she could get Mason in position to intercept Amanda before she reached the embassy, they stood a chance of stopping the leak in its tracks.

She started to dial Mason, but before she could finish, her phone rang.

"Good work, Helen," Jack mumbled. His tone was entirely different from their previous conversation, less than a half hour ago. The scotch was talking now.

"We'll have this thing shut down inside the hour, Jack."

"Fine." He hung up.

She got Mason on the line. "Okay. Our subjects are

traveling from the north of the city into the US embassy. They are due to arrive in one hour."

"Do you know their exact location?"

"Unfortunately, no. But we do know the time, and we know who they're going to meet."

"Do the original orders still stand?" Mason asked.

She rubbed her temples. "Yes. For the most part."

"For the most part? What the hell does that mean?" Mason demanded.

"The target is meeting with the deputy ambassador. Evidently, they're old friends..."

"So?"

"She requested a welcome party from the embassy Marines."

Silence. Then, "You're kidding?"

"Nope." More silence. "Are you still there, Mason?"

"Yeah. I was thinking. I'll have to take them before they reach the embassy, before they can request assistance."

"Do whatever it takes." She checked her screen. "I'm forwarding you their last known coordinates as well as their projected route." She pressed Send.

"Looks like you've got a clear choice," she muttered.

Mason grunted his acknowledgment. "I'll let you know the outcome."

The line went dead and Helen breathed a sigh of relief. *One last thing to do.* She opened up another program on her desk and started typing. A few seconds later, she was done, and she checked her spelling twice. Then she smiled.

The program was called TWANG, which stood for Terrorist Warning And Notification Grid. It was the government's newest emergency warning mechanism, a sort of electronic air raid siren.

Constructed shortly after 9/11, it had initially been deemed a failure. Most of that was poor perception, however. Until proven otherwise, people always felt they were faster than machines when it came to communications. It wasn't until two thwarted domestic terrorist attacks in late 2004 that the system gained wide acceptance.

Her message was simple:

US EMBASSY, PARIS, LIKELY TARGET OF ATTACK NEXT SIXTY MINUTES.
CONFIDENCE LEVEL: HIGH.

The message, while vague, would trigger an immediate lockdown at the embassy. Doors would be locked, windows would be shuttered, and all non-embassy personnel would be evacuated until the security staff had a chance to sweep the building and signal the all clear. Most importantly, it would ensure that Liza Barnett had no way to contact Kurt Vetter or Amanda Carter.

She read the message one more time, checking for typos, and then sent it into the ether. Satisfied, she got up from her chair and headed for the break room. She was looking forward to putting this all behind her, and getting back to the real mission.

Thirty-Four

L IZA COUGHED INTO HER HAND, then glanced at her clock. It was almost time. "I think that'll cover it," she said to her chief of staff, dismissing him.

The earnest young man, a recent transfer from the Kabul embassy, gathered his papers and left without a word, leaving her alone for the first time since her discussion with Amanda. She took a deep breath and picked up her desk phone. The whole time the staffer had been speaking, Liza had been rehearsing how she would alert the embassy to Amanda's arrival. It was a delicate balance. She had gotten the distinct impression from her friend that coming to the embassy was an act of last resort, and as such, she needed to exercise discretion about every aspect of her arrival.

Alert the guards too soon, and whoever was pursuing Amanda, if they were on the inside, would have time to cause problems. Alert them too late, on the other hand, and Amanda wouldn't even reach the front gate. This required a fine sense of balance.

She checked her watch again. *It's time.* A red light flashed on her phone. A moment later, her Blackberry vibrated madly, skittering across her desk like an angry crab.

She grabbed it and turned it over. The customary Blackberry applications weren't visible. In their place was a bright red screen filled with scrolling white text.

```
US EMBASSY, PARIS, LIKELY TARGET OF ATTACK
NEXT SIXTY MINUTES.
  CONFIDENCE LEVEL: HIGH.
  LOCKDOWN IN PROGRESS.
```

Liza's heart skipped a beat. Despite the air conditioner rattling away in the corner, she broke out in a heavy sweat. *What the hell?*

Her desk phone rang, startling her out of her paralysis. It was her boss, the ambassador.

"Rick," she answered.

"Liza. My phone is going crazy. What's going on down there?"

Liza and her boss, Richard Jensen, went back a long way. They had first been posted together in the embassy in Mexico City eight years earlier and had been tracking each other's careers ever since. So far, at least for Liza, working for him had been a wise career decision. Rick got to handle all of the high-level, external political bullshit, leaving her to work more behind the scenes and get the real work done.

"I don't know yet." She stepped out of her office and looked up and down the hallway. Staffers were running in every direction with frightened looks on their faces.

As she was about to return to her desk, she was almost flattened by a squad of Marines hustling down the hall. They bristled with weapons and communications gear. The looks on their faces told her this was no drill. She recognized one of the soldiers, a young woman from her home state of California. Liza shot her a reassuring look, but the woman didn't acknowledge her. The marines disappeared around the corner on their way to the front of the building. She was in a combat zone now.

"Lots of soldiers moving around here, Rick," she said into the phone. "I think something big is about to happen."

"Where are you?" Rick asked.

"My office."

"Fuck," Rick said, exasperated. "Be careful, Liza. And call me as soon as you learn anything. I'll be on the next train."

"Will do." She ended the call.

Overhead, an alarm shrieked, a high pitched tone that warbled like a dying cat. Liza covered her ears and dashed down the hall, heading for the operations center. She had to find out what in the hell was going on, who was threatening the embassy, and what she could do about it. Then she had to make herself visible to reassure the troops.

It's got to be Amanda, she realized as she ran. Someone, somehow, has learned of her arrival. They were shutting the embassy down, locking it tight so she couldn't come in. She cursed, frustrated at how powerless she felt.

She ducked into the next office and picked up a phone. She pressed nine to get an outside line and waited. Nothing. She toggled the phone. Still nothing.

Shit! She smacked her forehead. *Lock down.*

Outside communications were severed during the red alert. *My Blackberry*. It was sitting on her desk. She turned and raced for her office. She had to warn Amanda off before she drove into the gathering shit storm.

Another group of stone-faced soldiers jogged by as she turned the corner to her office. She went in, closed the door behind her, and thumbed the lock. A moment later, Amanda's phone was ringing. "Please, please answer," Liza pleaded as she watched her door.

Thirty-Five

With a frustrated sigh, Amanda snapped her laptop closed and stuffed it back into her bag. The search had been a bust. She and Kurt had been sitting in the hotel parking lot for the past half hour, leaching off of the free Wi-Fi signal. She had run through Nigel's decrypted data, plugging various strings of text into Google, hoping for some kind of hit.

The only bit of interesting data had been a book published by Jack Carson in 1989. It was a long out-of-print political rebuttal of the Communist system. *Useless.*

She snuck a quick glance at Kurt. Something about him intrigued her, something she couldn't quite put her finger on. He shifted in his seat, and she felt her face grow warm. She turned away, casting her gaze toward the hotel. *Now is not the time for that,* she scolded herself.

Her phone rang. She pulled it out and checked the display. "Liza," she mouthed.

She answered, "Liza?"

"Yeah... Listen—you need to back off. Something is happening here—I think someone knows you're coming in."

Amanda felt as if she had been punched in the gut. Liza was her last hope. She shot Kurt a distressed glance. "What do you mean? Where else can we go? We're out of options here!"

"I don't—" She heard a knocking sound, then loud banging on the other end of the line, as if someone was trying to break down a door.

"I've got to go," Liza choked out. "Be safe."

Amanda pulled the phone away from her ear and stared at the screen in shock. She looked over at Kurt.

"Who was it?" he asked, his voice full of concern.

"The embassy is out." Amanda stared off into the distance as she spoke, looking through Kurt, unable to meet his eyes.

"Out? What do you mean out?" He probed, obviously alarmed.

Amanda came back to the present. "I mean, I just spoke with Liza. Something is going down. She waved us off."

"Fuck!" Kurt slammed his palm against the dashboard.

Amanda's brow furrowed as she considered their options. There weren't many left. The UK was out. France was out. There was nowhere to go. *Well, maybe that isn't true.* "I've got an idea."

Kurt raised an eyebrow. "I hope it's better than this one."

That stung, but she couldn't blame him. Nothing was happening as she expected. "Well. Here's how I see it. We're out of options. Someone—the CIA, I assume—is at least one step ahead of us, maybe more."

"Uh huh," Kurt agreed, nodding.

"So far we've been depending on others for help, relying on the good will of the embassies. I think we need to readjust our expectations, our strategy. We need to take care of this ourselves."

Kurt jerked his head. "Do you mean go to Russia?"

Amanda nodded, slowly at first, and then with more conviction. "Exactly."

Kurt rolled his eyes. "Great idea, Amanda, except for one small detail; we're in Paris. We have less than twenty-four hours according to those files, and someone is trying to kill us. How do you propose we get to Russia?"

"Hire a private plane, a charter."

"Do you have—"

"Yeah. I have plenty of cash. And this way we'll avoid customs and immigration as well. All we need to do is bribe the right people as we enter the country, and we'll slip right through. Things may get a little dicey once we get on the ground, getting a car and all, but I'm sure we can figure it out."

Kurt cracked his knuckles, studying the backs of his hands. "Okay."

"You're sure?"

"Let's do it before I change my mind."

Amanda fired up the car.

Thirty-Six

KURT STRETCHED AND YAWNED, BUMPING Amanda in the process.

"Sorry," he murmured. They were on final approach to the Sheremetyevo civil aviation field, on the outskirts of Moscow. They had been in the air for a little over four hours.

"Tired?" Amanda asked with a soft smile.

He nodded and swallowed another yawn.

"Me too." Getting a spot on an unfilled charter had been a stroke of pure genius, he had to admit. He thought back to the realization that they couldn't enter the embassy, that they had been waved off, and grimaced. *What a disaster.* At the time, he had almost given up hope; it was the absolute worst thing he could have heard.

He checked his watch. *Three hours.* If Mike's data was accurate, that was all the time they had left until the city beneath him became a radioactive crater. And he and Amanda were heading right for the center of it.

Kurt checked himself. Intellectually, he knew he should be running the opposite direction, putting as much distance between himself and Moscow as possible. Yet, here he was. In the end, it was a simple calculation. Mike had died to get this information to him. Millions, maybe even billions, would die as well if he didn't act. That was the bottom line, regardless of whether he liked it or not. *Of course*, he thought, *it would have been nice to have some help; some backup in case things went to shit.* He sighed. *Screw it.*

The plane hit a patch of turbulence, and Kurt tightened his grip on his armrest. He didn't like flying in general, and he hated small planes in particular. Amanda patted his hand, sending chills up his arm. He still didn't know what to make of her. He was attracted to her, but now was not the time for that.

"Soon," she said.

"It can't be soon enough."

The plane, a Cessna Citation, carried three other passengers, a group of German and Russian executives on their way to Moscow for a meeting. Kurt didn't understand a word of their conversation, as he didn't speak either language. Amanda, as he had guessed, spoke both.

She had come up with the idea of booking seats on a charter. Before entering the offices of Air Europa, a small executive charter company based out of Charles de Gaulle Airport, she had pulled a large wad of Euros from her backpack and stuffed them into her front pocket. They were mostly hundreds. He assumed they were to be used to bribe, or encourage, someone to get them a spot on the airplane and a subsequent free pass into the Russian Federation.

He had assumed correctly. A few moments later, the woman behind the counter, a willowy young

Parisian, called out in Russian to the three men in the departure lounge. One of the men got up and waddled to the counter. A long guttural exchange had ensued; money changed hands, and five minutes later, Kurt and Amanda were boarding the Cessna with the businessmen.

On board, after settling into the front of the passenger cabin, they had shared some vodka to celebrate their trip. The others had sequestered themselves in the rear, speaking in boisterous tones.

Kurt felt a bump. *Gear down.*

"Landing gear," Amanda confirmed.

"Yep." He straightened in his seat and checked his seat belt.

Thirty seconds later, there was a loud chirp and another thunk as the landing gear met the runway. The plane bounced once. Twice. And then all three wheels were firmly planted on the tarmac. They rolled for what seemed like an eternity; Kurt stared out the window. This was his first time in Moscow, and he had a mental picture that he needed to reconcile. The Moscow of his imagination was a gray and dreary place, mostly constructed from images from old movies.

The plane slowed to a stop near a small terminal, and the light at the front of the cabin was extinguished. A cheer arose from the businessmen in the back, and Kurt and Amanda added their own weak hurrahs.

Collecting their meager belongings, they exited the aircraft by way of a set of portable stairs. Kurt inhaled, taking in the scent of a new city, as he walked down the stairs. At first whiff, it smelled like any other

European city. *Maybe a little more diesel*, he decided. Then he caught the scent of something different. He couldn't put his finger on it, but it made him wrinkle his nose.

Amanda didn't seem to notice. Come to think of it, she hadn't said much about her past experiences with Russia. He knew she had been here before, but had no idea for how long or what she had been doing. He decided it didn't really matter. She had said she didn't know anyone, didn't have any contacts, and that he would have to take her at her word.

"Let me do the talking," she said under her breath as they approached the terminal entrance.

In her right hand, she carried her backpack, stuffed with Euros, Pounds, and dollars.

Either it'll work, or it won't. If it doesn't, then we'll be thrown in jail and burned up in a few hours when the bomb goes off. He didn't like the worst case. He hoped it worked.

Best case, they'll take the bribe and wave us through. Then all we have to do is find the bomb and somehow deactivate it. He laughed to himself. *Long odds.*

They passed through the main portal and a blast of frigid, damp air assaulted them, making them both shiver. Kurt's impression was that the summer weather in Moscow was pretty close to that of his home in Virginia. Hazy, hot, and humid.

The arrival lounge contained a long counter along the back wall. It was relatively modern in construction, likely built during the post-communist construction boom of the early 1990s. Before that, he reasoned, there wasn't much call for international civil aviation.

Behind the counter, an obese middle-aged man was helping the other travelers. Their passports were arrayed on the counter, and the man was comparing names to paperwork and pounding a hand stamp on each document to record their entry.

A young woman appeared from a door on the right side of the room and slipped behind the counter. "*Da*," she said, waving them over.

Amanda approached the counter with a purposeful stride and leaned on it with her elbows. He stood slightly to the side and behind, trying to remain as inconspicuous as possible. For the next minute, Amanda and the woman conversed in rapid-fire Russian. The tone started to worry him. It appeared as if the women were arguing. There was an inordinate amount of gesturing and guttural noises. At one point, Amanda turned and pointed over her shoulder at the now-dormant aircraft and shouted what sounded like an expletive, albeit one that certainly didn't map to anything in the English language.

Finally, after what seemed an eternity, the woman sighed, and then motioned for Amanda to follow her into the back. Amanda gave Kurt's hand a quick squeeze. "Let me have your passport." He handed it to her, and she disappeared around the counter.

By this point, the other travelers were long-gone. Their agent was hunting and pecking on a shiny new computer terminal. Kurt wandered over to the grimy window overlooking the tarmac and gazed out at the airplane.

From there, he had a good vantage of the air traffic in and out of the civil field. The thing that most amazed him was the subtle differences in the aircraft from what he was accustomed to in the west. Many of the aircraft looked like they had been copied piece for piece, except for one minor, and sometimes major, detail to give them their own unique personalities.

The Russians were world-class engineers. Early in the days of the Cold War, they had become masters at copying Western designs, either through outright theft or through studious reverse engineering. Nevertheless, they hadn't been content to copy. They had learned from their efforts and, in some cases, their designs far exceeded the capabilities of their sources from the west. In general, the Russian aircraft were over-engineered, able to withstand much more abuse than their western counterparts.

The door squeaked opened behind him. He turned to see Amanda emerge, a faint smile playing on her lips. She gave him a discreet nod, and then turned back to the woman behind her. Another exchange ensued, this one lacking the vitriol of the earlier discussion. The women exchanged brief kisses on their cheeks, and Amanda turned back to him.

"We're all set."

"That's it?" Kurt asked with a raised eyebrow.

"That's it." She gave him his passport. "Put this somewhere safe."

"The car is out there," she said, pointing at a heavy metal door on the side of the building.

"Car?"

Amanda gave him a sly smile. "Included in the cost of admission."

Once again, Kurt was impressed by her endless resourcefulness. Who else could fly into Russia unannounced and waltz through customs, procure a car, and not break a sweat?

He followed her through the door and back into the heat of the afternoon.

Thirty-Seven

HELEN WAS SUFFERING FROM A serious case of hurry up and wait, and it was pissing her off. With less than two hours until the attack in Moscow, neither she nor Jack had heard from Fish, Mason still hadn't recovered the data, and to top it all off, Jack had summoned her to his office. *If Jack asks me one more time if I've heard from Fish, I'm going to fucking scream*, she thought as she marched down the hall.

"I'm sure everything is fine with him," she had told Jack in her calmest voice the last time he had checked in. "If Fish needs us, he'll call." That hadn't been enough. Jack was on edge like she had never seen before. And the scotch he had been swilling wasn't helping matters. He was a belligerent drunk, she realized, and it was all directed at her.

She was concerned about the absence of Fish's locator beacon. It was unusual, but not unheard of when an agent was deep undercover. The only thing she could hope to control was Mason's end of the operation—retrieving the data.

Helen was on the verge of panic. Kurt and Amanda had not been eliminated yet. Not only did it leave them all exposed if the data got out, but it looked bad for both her and Mason. After losing their prey in Paris because of a complete miscalculation on her part, she had put Mason into a holding pattern as she scrambled to determine where they had gone. Now, she was at a complete loss, her frustration raging like an open furnace.

Her gut told her they were probably on their way to Moscow. At the same time, her intellect told her Amanda was probably trying to contact another resource, someone else she could trust, in western Europe. She took a deep breath and cracked her knuckles. *There's no time.*

She reached Jack's door. It was closed. She knocked twice, short fast knocks.

"Come in!" he boomed.

Steeling herself, Helen entered. The first thing she noticed was the blinds. They were drawn. The next thing was the light. The overheads, bluish-white government-issue fluorescents, were off. A green-shaded accountant's lamp cast a pool of light on Jack's desk, and a floor lamp lit the far corner. The room seemed particularly gloomy, and it matched her mood perfectly.

"Come in, Helen. Take a seat," he said, waving her to a chair.

She did. She noticed the open bottle of scotch on his desk.

Jack saw her notice and said, "Want one?"

Helen shook her head. *Not this time.* "No thanks."

They sat there in silence for a moment until Helen

started to get uncomfortable. Jack was staring at her, but he seemed to be looking through her at the same time.

"Was there something specific you wanted to discuss?" she asked, unable to bear the silence any longer.

"Yes. There is."

Well, tell me then, she thought.

"Where do I begin?" His voice was low and conspiratorial.

She held her breath. Something had changed. Something about him—his body language, his eyes. She fixed her eyes on his, trying to read his thoughts.

Jacked straightened and loosened his tie. "There's no use beating around the bush here. Fish isn't in Moscow to assassinate the President."

"No?"

"The Chechens he's working with, they're a bit more resourceful than I've led you to believe." *Oh shit. Here it comes.*

Have you ever heard of Operation Track and Hold?" he asked.

It sounded familiar, but she couldn't place it. "Maybe."

"It was started in the early nineties, after the wall fell. The idea was to reduce the amount of nuclear weapons in the former Soviet republics by buying up their supply of fissile material, putting it into storage, and figuring out a way to track it going forward."

Helen realized she had heard of a program along those lines, but hadn't known its name. "Yes. I've heard of it. What about it?"

"The program has been pretty successful. There

hasn't been a single case of an intact nuke getting loose. Oh, there have been a few instances where small amounts of nuclear material, a little bit of uranium or a little bit of plutonium have disappeared, but nothing large enough to cause concern."

Helen had heard all of this before. "And?"

"Well, that's about to change," he said with a grim expression.

Helen was no idiot. She knew exactly where this was going. Chechens. CIA involvement in a program to decommission nukes. Fish. It all added up.

She opened her mouth to protest, but Jack silenced her with a wave.

"A year ago, Fish, Mike Vetter, and I came up with an idea. A plan, if you will, to eliminate our Russia problem once and for all. All we needed was a way to do it without looking like it was caused by us."

"Let me guess. The Chechens?" Helen was starting to feel sick to her stomach.

"Yes. We found a way to make a decommissioned SS-20 warhead disappear from the Clean Sweep system. The Soviets were never very good at tracking their weapons. As far as the international monitors can tell, the weapon never existed."

"How big is it?" Helen interrupted.

"Big. A hundred and fifty kilotons."

She sat back in her chair and ran her fingers through her hair. She felt short of breath, as if a giant were sitting on her chest. Visions of Moscow in ruins played across her mind's eye. Jack continued speaking, but she didn't hear. *Why is he telling me this? Why now? Is it because of Fish?*

After a moment, Jack must have realized he had

lost her. "Helen?"

"HELEN!" he yelled. "I need you here with me. Now!"

She snapped back into the present. Jack looked angry again, his earlier wistfulness only a memory.

He pointed at his watch. "In a little over two hours, this bomb is going to detonate in downtown Moscow. Once that happens, our job is going to get very interesting, very fast."

No kidding.

She opened her mouth to speak, but nothing came out. She didn't know where to start. This was so much bigger than she had ever bargained for. This was murder on a scale she could barely comprehend.

The next several minutes passed in a flash as Jack described his plan for during and after the attack.

Thirty-Eight

"HOW LONG?" KURT ASKED.

AMANDA checked the time on her cell phone and frowned.

"Two hours."

"Fuck!" he exclaimed. "Goddamn it!" They were sitting still in traffic on the Sheremetyevo access road. A half mile ahead, lights from emergency vehicles flashed. Traffic was stopped in both directions.

"Can you see anything?" she asked.

He shifted in his seat. "No. Not a goddamned thing."

They had been sitting in the same place for fifteen minutes, waiting for the accident to clear. Moscow traffic was unpredictable on a good day, Amanda had warned as they left the employee lot. On a bad day, it could be impenetrable. This looked like a bad one.

He wrung his hands, unable to stop thinking about the seconds ticking by. If the bomb went off according to plan, or if someone got an itchy trigger finger and set it off early... well, they were sitting at ground zero. Thinking maybe they could reverse course, find a different way into the center of the city, he checked his rearview mirror. It was impossible. They were hemmed in with concrete barriers on both sides and a never-ending line of cars and trucks to the front and the rear.

"It's only six, no, seven miles," Amanda said, consulting the map on her phone.

He closed his eyes for a moment and willed himself to relax. He knew she was right. He tried to think of what Mike would do in the same situation. Mike would never have allowed things to get this far out of control in the first place. Mike wouldn't have gotten himself into this type of situation. Mike had always been a meticulous planner, considering every angle and always having a backup strategy for whatever he did. Even this time.

Kurt thought back to summer camp in Montana when he was ten. After watching Jurassic Park for the first time, he and Mike had both become rabid dinosaur enthusiasts. Their parents, in a rare act of parental largesse, had decided that the best way to feed their curiosity was to send them on a three-week paleontology dig in the heart of fossil country. Each day at camp, the boys toiled for hours under the hot sun, digging and brushing the hard packed dirt, searching for fragments of long-extinct animals.

One day near the end of their final week, Kurt came across a remarkable cache of bone fragments. Being only ten, he decided he wanted to keep some, to take them home.

When he told Mike of his plan to take the bones, Mike was enthusiastic about the idea, and together they set to figuring out the best way to get the bones out of the pit and into their luggage undetected. At the last minute, Mike changed his mind. "It's wrong, Kurt," he explained. "These bones don't belong to us. We need to tell the scientists."

Kurt had thrown a fit. "But I found them! They're mine!" he whined.

What happened next was unexpected. Mike, in a voice Kurt had grown to both love and hate over the years, explained why it was wrong to take the fossils. He did it in clear terms that even Kurt's ten-year-old mind could comprehend. Kurt didn't like it, not at all, but Mike was able to convince him that it was better to leave the bones where they had found them, to return home empty-handed.

Three weeks later, on the morning before the first day of school, Mike had asked him, "Do you remember those dinosaur bones we found in Montana?"

Kurt did. He was still disappointed about not bringing anything back, at caving to his brother's insistence that they do the right thing.

"Close your eyes." Kurt did. He held his breath in anticipation.

"Go ahead, open them," Mike said a second later.

Kurt opened his eyes and saw a shoebox on the bed. Nike. Air Jordans. He placed his hand on the lid, his curiosity raging.

His pulse quickened. "Is it...?"

Mike smiled. "Go ahead."

Kurt pulled the lid from the box and there, in his bedroom, were the very same fossils from the dig in Montana—six small slivers of fossilized bone nestled on one of their mother's dish towels.

"How?" He looked up. "I thought..."

Mike just shook his head and smiled. Kurt picked up the largest fragment and held it in his palm. It had heft, and he couldn't help but imagine the animal that had once roamed the plains of Montana millions of years before.

"What will Mom and Dad say?"

"Don't worry about them. Do you like the fossils?"

Kurt nodded, unable to contain himself. How Mike had gotten the fossils out and why he didn't seem troubled by it was beyond Kurt's comprehension. What was apparent, for the first time, was his brother's ability to make things happen. Mike could do anything.

A horn blared behind them, jolting him back to the present. He sniffled. *Mike could do anything except stay alive.* He hadn't seen the fossils in years. He assumed they were somewhere in his parents' house. *I'll have to look for them the next time I'm there... if there is a next time.*

"We're moving!" Amanda exclaimed. "Look!" She pointed at the emergency lights, which were coming toward them. A moment later, a roll-top truck passed, going the opposite direction. On the back of the truck was a mangled Volkswagen sedan, the loser of the accident that had held them up. A minute later, the traffic jam lurched to life in a peristaltic spasm.

Amanda ground the car into first and eased forward. "Are you ready for this?"

Kurt gave her a weak smile and nudged the duffel bag at his feet. "As ready as I can be. You?"

"Same."

They were both silent for the next few minutes. Amanda navigated through the herky-jerky Moscow traffic, looking for their exit. It was farther away than Kurt had expected.

After a series of turns, they found themselves on the edge of an old warehouse district. The address in Mike's data was several blocks ahead. Amanda slowed and pulled to the side of the road. She dropped it into neutral and left the engine running. "Well…"

"What are we waiting for?" he asked.

She stared straight ahead. "I need a second…"

While he waited, a plane flew over on its final approach to the airport. It was so low the windows of the car vibrated and rattled in their frames. That seemed to do it for Amanda. She snapped out of her trance, slipped the car back into gear, and pulled forward with a determined look.

Their plan, if crashing a warehouse full of militants could be called a plan, was about to be put to the test.

Thirty-Nine

ELEN STARED AT HER SCREEN, the letters and numbers dancing in random patterns, not making any sense. She couldn't focus. Not anymore. She changed her network switch to the public internet, and Googled 'blast radius calculator.' She clicked the first result, one of over five hundred.

She plugged in '150 Kilotons,' found Moscow on the supplied map, dropped a pin on the center of the Russian capitol, and clicked Submit. Three concentric shaded circles appeared on the map. The darkest, focused on an area about a mile and a half in diameter, showed complete devastation. All structures, without exception, would be reduced to rubble. The next circle, which extended out another mile, indicated major destruction, including obliteration of poorly-built structures and intense damage from the blast wave. The final circle was the one in which she was most interested. It was a given that anyone in the first two circles would die in the blast, but the third circle was much larger, extending almost all the way to the Third Ring, the outer beltway encircling the city. The blast calculator wasn't specific, but she knew that anyone within this zone who survived would wish they hadn't.

She closed the browser, tapping her mouse with her index finger as she thought of her next steps. The implications of Jack's plan were staggering. She couldn't begin to put a figure on the human toll, not to mention the economic impact the blast would have on Russia. And the rest of the world.

But... At the same time, it was genius. With one blast, they were going to eject Russia from the world stage forever; reduce them to a middling third world country, where they belonged.

But what if? Helen thought. *What if what was left of the Russian government figured out who was behind the bomb? That the CIA had orchestrated the whole thing? She felt queasy. If they realize it was us...*

She dialed Mason. "Where are you now?" she demanded without even saying hello.

"Charles de Gaulle. I'm waiting for a flight to Moscow."

Helen squeezed her eyes shut. She couldn't shake the image of a roiling mushroom cloud hovering over Moscow. Bodies burned to a crisp. A glowing crater filled with rubble. "No."

"Huh?"

"I said 'no.' Don't go."

He laughed. "And why wouldn't I go, Helen? Isn't that the most logical place for Vetter and Carson?"

"It is, yes. And—it's complicated. You have to trust me, Mason. Don't go to Russia, not today. In fact, if I were you, I would get as far away from major population centers as I could." She checked the time and felt her pulse quicken. "And fast, within the next hour."

Mason didn't respond. She could hear other people in the background and the announcer on the loudspeaker, first in French, and then repeating a message in a host of other languages. "Are you still there?"

"What's going on, Helen?" His voice had changed. Gone was the jocular do-anything-anytime Mason of a few moments ago. He was all business.

"I'm sorry. I can't say any more. But you have to get as far away as possible." *Maybe he'll listen.* She held her breath, hoping against hope.

"Okay."

"You'll do it?"

"What about Vetter and Carter?" That was a good question. She couldn't abandon the search, even though in a couple of hours it wouldn't matter anymore. If they were in Moscow, the problem would solve itself.

"Screw them! Just go! I'll be in contact."

She heard him swallow hard. "Okay, then. I don't know what this is all about, but I'll trust you."

Helen choked back an impulse to blurt out the truth. "Be safe."

"You, too." The line went dead.

She switched back over to the secure network and pulled up a web page showing the current DEFCON, or Defense Condition. The scale ranged from one to five, with five being the lowest and one meaning missiles were in the air. The screen said four, as it had for years. *No one else knows.*

Helen closed the browser and stood. She had a decision to make, a decision that would define the rest of her life.

Forty

"**H**EY, CHARLIE! I'VE GOT SOMETHING interesting here. Can you take a look?"

Darlene Foster pushed back from her desk to make room. She was pretty in a librarian-sort of way, with shoulder-length blond hair tucked behind her ears and smart horn-rimmed glasses.

"Hold on." Charlie Howell, her supervisor at the NSA, was finishing the last few words of a report, banging away on his keyboard with machine gun efficiency.

Darlene took a sip of her Diet Coke and waited. At the tender age of twenty-nine, she was one of the most proficient counter-intelligence analysts on Charlie's team. Her primary responsibility was monitoring the traffic between domestic government agencies and military units, searching for potential security breaches and evidence of espionage. Charlie's division had been created by secret presidential directive after a devastating string of intelligence leaks that had all but decimated the credibility of the Director of National Intelligence. In short, she was the watcher who watched the watchers.

She wasn't a typical analyst. For one thing, she had a PhD in predictive analytics from MIT. She could have been working on Wall Street, pulling down ten times her government salary, but instead she chose government service in an idealistic bid to make the world a better place. To date, she had been responsible for identifying three cases of improper information transfer and one bona fide case of espionage. The data breaches were dealt with through organizational process improvements, resulting in improved security for the agencies involved. The espionage case, however, had underscored her true value to the community and cemented her place in the NSA.

An Army major based in Afghanistan had turned and was feeding information to Taliban insurgents about U.S. troop movements. The traitor had done an admirable job at disguising his activities. He made sure his handlers didn't target every patrol, instead working with the Taliban to choose their attacks based on the output of a simple random number generator. The scheme had worked for six months and resulted in the deaths of seventeen U.S. soldiers. The military and the local CIA presence were flummoxed at the Taliban's ability to appear out of nowhere, and then disappear without a trace. Troops were added, and drone patrols were stepped up, both to no avail.

It wasn't until Darlene was tasked with monitoring traffic in the region that she picked out a pattern, a pattern the automated systems had missed. The break came when she noticed that a particular unit was requesting an unusual number of patrol briefings from far-flung units across the countryside. The number was barely above the statistical average, but it was enough to draw her eye.

Requesting patrol briefings in itself wasn't out of the ordinary. The Army spent considerable effort learning from ongoing operations, always striving to become more efficient. But this was different. As Darlene dug deeper, she discovered additional, more subtle anomalies in the pattern of requests, anomalies that were not consistent with the data from other operations. She had put a watch on the major's communications activities and two weeks later the traitor was in custody. She had no idea where he was now.

"Sorry about that. What have you got?" Charlie asked, putting a hand on her shoulder. Charlie was an old-school manager, touchy-feely with everyone under his command. Darlene had flinched the first time he touched her, but once she learned he acted that way with all of his employees, she had relaxed. The knowledge that Charlie had been happily married for thirty-five years and had seven grown children had helped put her mind at ease.

"Check it out," she said, pointing at the screen.

He leaned closer. "Hmmm." He scratched his jaw.

"It's a mobile phone intercept between two CIA agents; one is a woman named Helen Bartholomew. The other is a man named Mason Perot. She's in the states, and he's in France."

Charlie read the transcript silently, his lips moving. "Shit!" he exclaimed. "Those dumb bastards at the CIA. When will they ever learn?"

Darlene grinned. She was right. It *was* something. "I think we need to bump this one up, Charlie." He bobbed his head, considering her recommendation.

She continued, "She's telling him to stay away from cities. And this stuff about Moscow—I've got a real bad feeling."

"Have you run the reverse crawler?"

She glanced at the corner of the screen where a green progress bar was sitting at ninety percent. "It's almost done."

The crawler was a piece of software that analyzed historical signal traffic and looked for patterns. Due to the amount of signal traffic in the system at any given moment, the crawler was only useful when performing a targeted analysis. In this case, she had configured it to examine the traffic between these CIA agents using several keywords from the transcript and going back in time for a period of six weeks. The crawler would search archived data records for matches and perform an analysis of their relevance to the initial terms. The beauty of the crawler was that it would follow links automatically, expanding out from the initial terms to create a web of related activity.

Her computer beeped. The crawler was finished. She double-clicked the report and began to read. Charlie bent in to read over her shoulder. Two paragraphs into the report, he sucked in a breath and sank into an empty seat beside her.

"Oh, my God," he whispered.

Darlene couldn't speak. The information on the screen pointed to a massive conspiracy, one that stretched back years, within the CIA.

Charlie stood and checked his watch. "We have to call the President right now."

She flushed. *Call the President?* This is big.

Forty-One

PRESIDENT RICK COOPER, A LANKY man of fifty-one, with thick, wavy hair completing its journey from sandy brown to lustrous silver, was huddled over his desk reviewing a stack of pending legislation when there was a sharp knock on the door. He sat up straight and removed his reading glasses.

"Come in!" he bellowed, lamenting the reality of the office. He had no time to himself in this job. Even when everything around him appeared calm, his priorities could change in a heartbeat.

The door swung open and his national security advisor, Dominic Velasquez, entered his office. From the look on Dominic's face, Rick knew he wasn't stopping in to talk about last night's Yankees game. He and Dominic went all the way back to Yale. Thrown together in a cramped dorm room during their first year of college, they had become lifelong friends.

It was an unusual pairing. Rick, the son of a dentist from suburban Memphis, was a dyed-in-the-wool Republican raised in a comfortable upper middle class household where college and a professional career were guaranteed. Dominic, on the other hand, hailed from South Tucson, where his undocumented parents fought and scraped to build a better life for themselves and their American-born son. It wasn't until he reached the age of twelve that he fully comprehended the plight of his family, and his political allegiances were set in stone after seeing how his parents were treated.

It was odd that they got along so well, but at the same time, it made a certain sort of sense. Rick had a natural affinity for a crowd, and an innate ability to bridge the divide between disparate groups of people. This served him well through, first, the state legislature of Tennessee, then as a two-term governor, and finally, two years earlier, in his bid for the presidency. Along the way, he and Dominic had kept in touch.

Dominic had taken a different course. After a master's degree in criminal justice and a law degree with honors from Harvard, he had landed a spot inside the newly-formed Department of Homeland Security, heading up the Immigration and Customs Enforcement policy division and trying to right the wrongs that had shaped his experiences as a child.

Three months into his campaign, Rick had paid a visit to his old friend and presented an offer he couldn't refuse. Dominic, seeing a chance to do even more good from the inside, made the pragmatic decision to put his politics on the back burner and go to work for the man who he was sure was about to obtain the keys to the kingdom that was the United States.

"I just got this," Dominic announced, waving a

sheaf of papers in his left hand.

He gestured for Dominic to take a seat. "What is it, Dom?"

"Our friends over at Fort Meade picked up an intercept between two CIA agents. One here in the US and one in..." he glanced at his papers. "France." Dominic took a deep breath, and Rick noticed a thin bead of sweat on his forehead, surprising since Dominic ran marathons in his spare time. He motioned for him to continue.

"This comes from the group that uncovered that double agent in Afghanistan, by the way. Anyway, they ran it through their computers looking for patterns, and the damn thing lit up like a Christmas tree!"

Rick steeled himself for what was to come next.

"Something big is about to go down in Moscow. The agent at Langley was busy telling her counterpart in Paris to get out of town, to avoid cities at all cost. She said, and I quote, 'You have to get as far away as possible.'"

"From what?" he asked.

"That's the million dollar question, Rick, but we think it has something to do with Moscow. This week is their annual summit conference. All of the military leaders, the politicians, and the legislature are in town."

He ran his fingers through his hair. "Shit!"

"Yeah. And I've saved the best for last. Whatever this is, it's set to happen in about an hour and a half."

"Have you told anyone else?"

Dominic shook his head. "Not yet. I got this about ten minutes ago."

"Good. Here's what I want you to do. Get on the

phone and get the National Security Council, Defense, CIA, State, Homeland—everyone , and tell them to get their asses to the situation room as fast as they can. Next…"

"Uh, Rick. I think Buzz is in Afghanistan this week," Dominic said, referring to the Secretary of Defense, Bill "Buzz" Dumfries.

"Get his deputy then, but get word to Buzz that something's up."

Dominic checked his watch. "I think everyone else is in town. I'll scramble them."

"Okay. Meanwhile, I'm going to make a few calls, see what else I can learn."

"Anything else?"

Rick stared at the ceiling for a moment. "No. That's it."

Dominic got up and turned to leave.

"Dominic?"

"Yes?"

"Do you think this is real?"

Dominic considered his response for a moment, and then nodded. "It sure looks that way, Rick."

"Okay. I'll see you in a few."

Dominic exited the room, the door snicking closed behind him.

Rick circled back around his desk and stacked the papers he had been reviewing, placing them in a folder with red stripes on the front.

The shit was in the air and heading toward the fan.

Forty-Two

KURT STOPPED SHORT, CAUSING AMANDA to bump into him from behind.

"What is it?" she asked, unable to see around him.

Having left their car two blocks back, they were crouched behind the burnt-out shell of an old city bus. Approaching on foot, they both had agreed, was the best and only way to maintain any sense of surprise.

He held up his hand. He thought he had seen something in an upper window of the warehouse, some movement. *Maybe a person.* The sun was on the far side of the building throwing a long shadow across the fractured, weed-covered street. He concentrated on the window high above, holding his breath while he watched for the movement again.

After counting to twenty, he exhaled and whispered, "I thought I saw something."

The warehouse was three stories with a flat roof. Metal catwalks connected by steep rusty stairs circled the building on the top two floors. Facing them was a large set of rolling metal doors. Standing at least twenty feet tall, the doors were large enough to swallow all but the largest vehicle. The only sound was the low roar from the highway several blocks over. Kurt motioned Amanda forward, and she came to his side.

Together, they listened, hoping to hear some sign of life, some confirmation that they were in the right place.

"It's like no one is home," Amanda whispered. "I'd expect more activity this close to detonation."

Kurt shrugged. He wasn't sure what to expect. He checked his watch. *One hour and twenty minutes.* "Shit!" he hissed. He held his watch so Amanda could see it.

She closed her eyes and muttered something under her breath, a prayer perhaps.

Screwing up his courage, Kurt took a step from the cover of the bus. He held his breath, counted to twenty, then checked the warehouse windows for motion. He took another breath and waited again. His hands were shaking as he wiped a bead of sweat from his forehead. After two more steps, with no sign of anyone above and no crack of a rifle followed by sudden, blinding pain, he decided they were in the clear. The movement he had seen had been a trick of the light. *It had to be.*

"I think we're clear," he whispered over his shoulder. He was standing in the open, an easy target for anyone on the roof.

Convincing Amanda he should take the lead had been a nightmare. "I have to," he had pleaded. "It's because of me, because of Mike, that we're here. You've done so much getting us to Russia, finding a car—let me do this one thing. She had relented, but not before giving him systematic instructions on how to probe the defenses without getting killed.

Separating them from the nearest ladder on the warehouse was a wide-open stretch of asphalt. A hundred meters, he guessed, maybe a little more. It was that way around the entire structure. They had chosen this side because of the shadow; it was the only cover available.

He sprinted for the nearest ladder with his head down, arms pumping, running on the balls of his feet in order to make as little sound as possible. Amanda followed close on his heels. He ran faster than he had ever run before, so hard he saw stars in his eyes, and his side felt as if it was about to split apart. Twenty meters short of the stairwell, the big door in the center of the building rumbled open.

Kurt watched in terror as light flooded the interior of the space. *They can see us*, he thought. He ran faster. They made it just as the throaty roar of a revving engine split the air. Slipping around the edge of the building, out of sight of anyone coming from the front, they pressed their backs against the warm corrugated metal wall and panted, exhausted by the run.

Inside the building, the engine revved several times, and then it moved away from them. They pressed harder against the wall, trying to disappear. All it would take was for the vehicle to take a left turn, and they would be discovered. Out of the corner of his eye, Kurt caught a flash of metallic blue as a late model Porsche Cayenne shot from the building and took a wide turn to the right, away from them. The noise of the engine faded as the SUV raced away, and the doors rumbled closed.

Kurt and Amanda shared a look of relief. He could see it in Amanda's eyes, the same thing he was feeling—they had barely escaped with their lives. They waited until the doors clanged shut and then made their way to the fire ladder hanging down from the second floor. Kurt dropped to one knee, laced his fingers together into a step, and boosted Amanda up.

A minute later, they were on the third floor catwalk.

Forty-Three

"**I**S THIS EVERYONE?" PRESIDENT COOPER asked, disappointed at the turnout.

Spaced around the long oval table in the situation room were the Deputy Secretary of Defense, Daniel Bickenstaff; the Secretary of State, Hazel Bingham; the Secretary of Homeland Security, Mark Djini; and the Director of the CIA, Paul Pungley. Darlene Foster and Charlie Howell, representing the NSA, sat in chairs along one wall, along with a smattering of staffers from the other agencies. The Secretary of Defense and several other staffers were on the phone.

Dominic put his water glass on the table. "I think so, sir. We have a few inbound—General Richter, Admiral Milken, and a few others—but this is it for the moment."

Rick gave a quick nod, then stood and cleared his throat. "Ladies and gentleman. We've got a big problem here." He directed his eyes at the Director of the CIA.

"About an hour ago, our people at Fort Meade came across some information that leads me to believe something big—an attack—is about to occur in Moscow." He picked up a small gray remote control from the table and clicked a button in the center. Nothing happened. He tried again, pressing harder. Still nothing. He cursed. "Dom? Can you take a look at this?"

Dominic took the control, which drove the projector mounted on the ceiling, and started fiddling with it. There was a beep overhead, and the screen on the far wall turned blue as the projector came to life. Dominic handed the control back him.

"Thanks, Dom." He pushed the button on the remote, and an annotated transcript appeared on the far wall. It was the final conversation between Helen and Mason from a little over an hour earlier.

"This is what started it all," he said. "It's a conversation between a CIA controller in Washington and a field agent in Paris." He clicked the remote.

"And here's what we found when we started digging." The next several screens displayed a trace of all of the connections radiating out from both Helen and Mason, including Jack Carson, Mike Vetter, and Fish Coldwell.

All eyes in the room shifted to the Director of the CIA. He sat up straight in his seat, gritted his teeth.

"Now, if you look at the timestamps," Rick continued, "you'll notice this information is fresh. That's a testament to the hard work of Charlie and his staff." He gestured at Charlie and Darlene. Charlie gave a slight nod while Darlene blushed.

The deputy director of the Department of Defense started to speak, but Rick held up his hand, cutting him off. "Relax, Daniel. Before you jump to conclusions, I've already spoken with Paul." He gave the director a slight nod of encouragement. "Can you give the rest of us a briefing on what's going on inside CIA?"

"Yes, Mr. President." Paul Pungley, fifty-seven, was a career CIA bureaucrat. He wasn't Rick's first choice for the job, nor his second or third. He knew the agency inside out and had been there long enough to know where the bodies were buried and who had buried them. An unimaginative man, he preferred to delegate the majority of his duties to his staff and ride on their accomplishments. In one respect, he was exceptional—responding to a crisis. Paul was fabulous as ferrying out the minutest detail about an issue and holding people accountable for their actions. At this moment, there was no one else Rick would rather have had in the hot seat.

"Things are changing fast, but this is what we have so far. We've uncovered a rogue element within the agency. They appear to have established links to a group of radical Chechen separatists, and I, we, believe they have been collaborating with these same Chechens to arrange for an attack on Moscow." The room exploded with the sound of a dozen voices, all vying to have their questions answered.

Rick motioned for everyone to be patient. "Let Paul continue, please."

Paul did. He spent the next two minutes describing what his team had learned about Jack's organization, its history and its goals.

"Isn't this week the annual meeting of the congress and the Russian military?" the Secretary of State asked.

"It is," the director responded. "And that's one of the reasons we're so worried. As we speak, the President, the Prime Minister, most of the senior military leadership and their congress are all in Moscow." The room went quiet for a minute as the participants digested the news. The world had been a quiet place for the past several years. The administration had been working to repair the damage, both political and economic, of the Iraq and Afghanistan wars, and most people's attention had shifted to domestic concerns. That was over now.

From six thousand miles away, Buzz's voice came through the speakerphone in the center of the table. "I suggest we go from DEFCON three to two right away."

The Secretary of DHS said, "I agree, but I believe the terrorist threat level should remain the same. We don't want to scare people unnecessarily."

"I disagree," Dominic piped up. "I think we should raise the terrorist threat level as well."

From there, the conversation descended into a free-for-all, as the people around the table and on the phone brainstormed an appropriate response. He let this proceed for a good two minutes before weighing in. "That's enough," he said, his voice cutting through the fray. "I've heard what I need." The bickering stopped and everyone turned their attention towards their commander-in-chief.

"I need a few minutes to gather my thoughts. We'll reconvene in ten." He pushed back his chair and stood. The others followed suit.

"And Paul," he added.

"Yes, Mr. President?"

"I want an update on the people responsible for

this as soon as you have them in custody."

The spy boss gave a sharp nod. "Yes, sir. They're being picked up as we speak."

He dismissed the meeting. The situation room was two hundred feet below the white house proper, buried in a watertight, shock- and blast-proof capsule deep in the Potomac water table. The name belied the magnitude of the facility. Rather than a single room, there were over fifty, ranging from private quarters to planning and command and control centers for various agencies. The total square footage far exceeded that of the executive building on the surface.

Before Dominic could go, he put a hand on his shoulder, stopping him. "Dom. Can I speak to you in private for a minute?"

"Yes, Mr. President. What is it?"

Rick ignored the looks from the other members of the his cabinet. They all understood the special bond between him and his National Security Advisor, and they all resented it. Dom had his ear on all matters.

He and Dominic stood in place while the others filed out. When the door finally *thunked* shut, he gestured to Dominic. "Have a seat."

Dominic did, with a worried look on his face.

"I heard a lot of conflicting opinions here. I understand all of the various positions, but I'm disturbed. Most people seem concerned with punishing those fools over at the CIA who started this."

Dominic sighed. "I know. It's a natural reaction." He checked his watch and raised his eyebrows at Rick.

"I know. I know. We don't have shit for time. Have I ever told you that that's my least favorite thing about this job? Everything is always a goddamned emergency, always has to have happened yesterday." He shook his head and sat on the edge of the table. "The one thing I kept thinking," he continued, "was what about the Russians? Everyone is focused on our reaction. "I'm considering calling President Sokolov and spilling the whole thing to him. There's nothing we can do from here, but they may be able to get some people in place, if we're lucky, and do something."

"Yes," Dominic said. "However, we need to be careful. If the Russians perceive we were somehow complicit in this attack, regardless of whether it was sanctioned, they may decide to retaliate preemptively, to hit us before we hit them."

He raised an eyebrow. "Do you think? Sokolov seems like a reasonable man." He had met him a handful of times, at international meetings of the G8 and in an ongoing session of talks tasked with reducing the number of strategic nuclear weapons.

"It's a distinct possibility. Put yourself in their shoes. What if Sokolov called you and told you a bomb was about to go off in..." Dominic checked his watch, "an hour and five minutes and wipe out your entire government. Wouldn't you want to hit back? To take them with you?"

Rick thought this over, then stood. "Okay. Thanks, Dom."

Dominic straightened. "That's it, sir?" He adjusted his tie.

"Yes. That's it. I'll consider your guidance as I make my decision. Please tell the others it will be a few more minutes."

"I'll be outside then" Dominic said. He headed for

the door but stopped before opening it. "Rick?" he asked.

"Yes?" Rick looked up from the polished wood table.

"I'm sure you'll do the right thing."

Rick gave him a grim smile before turning back to his notes.

Forty-Four

HELEN'S MIGRAINE WAS COMING BACK. Starting at the base of her neck and reaching up and through her skull, it was coring its way into the center of her skull with long, icy fingers. Stress, she told herself. Since her conversations with Mason and Jack, she had been at a loss for what to do. According to the clock, there was only a little over an hour until the fireworks in Moscow. She had one hour until life as she knew it was over.

She massaged her neck with her left hand, digging at the knotted muscles, trying to break up the stress and head off the headache before it took root. She groaned. It was no use. Her neck was a knotted rope of iron.

Her thoughts drifted back to Mike Vetter. He had always been one of her favorites. A field officer with years of experience and an innate understanding of the Russian mind, he had been the last person that she had ever expected to turn traitor. Now she understood. *How could I have missed it?* she asked herself, cursing her blindness. *Why did I sit by and let that happen? Why did I trust Jack?* All of these questions and more flashed through her mind in a painful blur and then, in an instant, she knew what she had to do.

She had to leave. *Right now.* She had to follow the same advice she had given to Mason. *Jack can go to hell. This isn't what I signed up for.* She picked up her car keys, hesitated, and then put them down again.

Her hand went to her mouse. She had one more thing to check... She clicked on her desktop. Her computer screen went blank. The border flashed bright red. A white message appeared in the center of the screen. *Access Restricted.* Helen clicked her mouse again, to no avail. Someone had locked her out of the system.

They know. Her heart skipped a beat as she considered the implications of her actions, of taking the fall for her involvement. In a flash, she grabbed her car keys and her badge and bolted from her desk. Stopping at the door, she composed herself, tucking her hair behind her ears and putting as much of a smile on her lips as she could muster. There was no way, she knew, she could hide the ghostly pallor that colored her skin.

She opened the door and exited the secure space. She would have to pass Jack's office on the way out. The main exit was a set of turnstiles and backscatter body scanning machines manned by very serious men with their fingers on their triggers. Ever since the incident with the distraught Iraqi refugee looking for his missing relatives two years earlier, security had been on high alert. Prior to that event, it had been a simple matter of waving at the guards she saw on average four times a day and swiping her badge through a reader. No longer. Now the guards scanned everyone on the way into the facility and routinely, although seemingly at random, scanned some on the way out. The agency took no chances with its employees and the secrets in their heads.

Helen stared down the hall. A two-minute walk on a normal day, it now seemed as if the guard shack was a million miles away. She set off at a slow walk, taking pains to control her speed, trying not to break out into a full-bore run that would overwhelm her exercise-deprived body and leave her breathless and panting at the guard station, ready for a thorough interrogation.

As she passed Jack's office, she noted light leaking from underneath the door. She kept moving, picking up her pace. Three minutes later, she was outside. She had passed through the guard shack unmolested despite her fears. The order to shut off her computer access had obviously not wound all the way through security yet. She strode across the parking lot to her Honda Accord and slid behind the wheel.

The engine fired up with a muted roar and she backed out of her space. Feeling a bit more confident, Helen threw the car into drive and started forward. She had one more hurdle to pass before she was in the clear. After that, she had no idea. She couldn't go home. She couldn't go to the bank. She had maybe two hundred dollars in her purse.

But Helen knew people. A lot of people. She had a brief mental image of her face splashed across CNN with the words 'Wanted for genocide' floating underneath. She pushed the thought aside. *I'll deal with that later. For now, I have to get to the interstate.*

Then I'll have options.

She rolled up to the gate. Swallowing hard, she took a deep breath. Edward, one of the daytime parking lot guards, sidled up to her car making a circular motion with his index finger, telling her to roll down the window. She did.

"Leaving early today, Ms. B.?"

"Yes. I have some personal business." She flashed him her most innocent smile.

"Well, have a good—"

He cocked his head, straightened, took a step back, and drew his pistol. Helen's insides turned to water. *Radio.* A little white wire curled up and over Edward's ear, disappearing into his ear canal. *Goddamn it!* Out of the corner of her eye, she saw flashing lights approaching in her rear view mirror. Next, she heard the sirens.

"Step out of the car, Ms. Bartholomew," he ordered, his voice devoid of all emotion.

"I don't understand, Edward," she pleaded. "I'm late for my appointment." She stole a glance at the guard booth and saw the other guard speaking urgently into a radio and gesturing wildly with his hands. Meanwhile, the lights were getting closer.

Helen closed her eyes and crossed herself, then she pressed the accelerator to the floor. Two years earlier, before the government had installed the pop-up, that might have worked, but not now. The barriers, monolithic blocks of concrete and rebar, were embedded in every street leading into and out of the campus. Each barrier was mounted on a system of rails and relied upon shaped explosive charges to raise it into a defensive position with the push of a button.

Once raised, they were strong enough to prevent an eighteen-wheeler traveling at eighty-five miles per hour from getting through.

There was an ear-splitting bang and, ten feet in front of her car, a solid wall appeared out of thin air. Her Honda was no match. The last thing she saw before passing out was her airbag exploding from her steering wheel.

~ * * *~

Jack swirled his scotch and watched the amber liquid race around the glass, unable to escape its confines. *So this is it?* He thought with a twinge of melancholy. He had just gotten off the phone with a well-placed contact in the director's office. The staffer, a former employee who owed him a favor, had warned him the big boss was on his way over, and that he was loaded for bear. He took a sip, savoring the smoky burn of the liquid on his lips. There was only one reason the director would come to him—he had been discovered.

He checked his watch. Fifty-five minutes until detonation. *There's no way to stop it now.* A faint smile played on his lips. He pulled his secure mobile phone from his jacket pocket, flipped it open, and traced his fingers across the keyboard.

There was a contingency plan, instituted by Mike Vetter, of all people. Before delivering the bomb to the Chechens, Fish had wired in a backdoor detonator connected to the guts of a mobile phone. Only three people knew the code. Jack was the last one left alive. All he had to do was dial a local Virginia telephone number, and the global communications network would route the call to wherever the bomb was located, triggering the onboard detonator. It was an insurance policy of sorts, a way to prevent the rebels from backing out of their end of the agreement.

Jack punched in the number and positioned his thick calloused thumb over *Send*. He hesitated, thinking of Fish, of all of their times together.

He closed his eyes and pressed *Send*. With an enormous *bang*, his door burst open, and a squad of marines in full battledress uniforms poured through, guns raised and pointed at him.

"Get your hands in the air right now!" one of the marines shouted. Jack froze, his mobile phone clenched in his palm. He eyed the young man. *He can't be more than twenty.*

He raised his hands, and out of the corner of his eye, he noticed another man lurking outside his door.

"Paul?" he called out. "Why don't you come on in?" The marines exchanged confused glances, but their weapons didn't waiver.

Director Pungley, flanked by his second in command, stepped through the twisted remains of Jack's door. "Jack," he said, his voice laced with contempt.

Jack held his chin up and forced a defiant sneer onto his face. "I did it for us all Paul. To finish what we fought so hard for."

The director frowned, obviously catching on to Jack's use of the past tense. "What do you mean you '*did* it'?" he asked, a look of horror spreading across his face.

Jack felt a divine sense of peace wash through his

body. He said nothing.

The director turned to the Marine captain. "Take this man into custody. Get him downstairs now." Downstairs, Jack knew, meant the interrogation facility in the third sub-basement. He had never been there himself, but had heard stories. *Whatever.*

The marines acted, one advancing on each side while the other two covered him. The marine on Jack's left pulled a nylon zip-tie from a clip on his belt and started to bend it into shape. "Hands on the desk, sir," the marine ordered. Jack leaned forward as if to comply, and then, as fast as he could, slipped his left hand under his desk to where his Colt 1911 was strapped. It wasn't uncommon for agency personnel to stash personal weapons in their offices; they faced the constant threat of personal violence over the course of most of their careers, and it was a hard habit to discard, even in the relative safety of CIA headquarters. Jack was no different.

He pulled the gun out and thumbed off the safety.

"Weapon!" the marine on his left shouted.

"Drop it now, sir!" the marine on the other side of his desk ordered. He hiked his gun a little tighter, focusing it squarely on Jack's chest.

"I'll save you the trouble," Jack said without emotion. He jammed the barrel into the soft flesh under his chin and pulled the trigger.

Forty-Five

KURT AND AMANDA FLOATED AROUND the catwalk, heading towards a nondescript metal door with a wire-reinforced glass window set at shoulder height. Kurt peered through the window, but it was so dirty he couldn't see anything. "So far, so good," he whispered.

Amanda gave him a supportive wink. He placed his hand on the doorknob and gave it a twist. It moved slightly in his grip, and then with a soft chunk, spun all the way around. "Shit!" He released the knob, as if burned.

They stood there holding their breath, waiting for some reaction to the sound. When, after a moment, nothing happened, he proceeded. Placing his left hand on the center of the door, he pulled on the handle with his right. It swung open an inch, enough to allow him to look inside.

The factory was dark and gloomy. Weak light filtered down through dingy skylights set into the roof, providing minimal illumination of the interior. From inside, he heard the low hum of voices speaking in a language he had never heard. *Probably Chechen or whatever they speak there.*

He pulled the door open a few more inches, and they slipped through. He eased the door closed behind them until it seated in the frame with a soft click. An identical catwalk ran around the interior of the building. Twenty feet from the chipped and stained concrete floor below, it provided a birds-eye view of the entire space. Several large machines of indeterminate function occupied one end of the room. The machines were large, over ten feet tall and painted puke-green. They looked abandoned.

"What are those?" he whispered, thinking perhaps that they were part of the bomb.

"I have no idea. Maybe they're some kind of electrical generators?"

It wasn't important. The other half of the factory was much more interesting. Inside the roll-top door was a battered black Mercedes Sprinter with blacked-out windows. Two men sat smoking on the floor nearby. A third man was typing on a laptop computer at a small wooden table.

He heard what sounded like another voice, maybe two, coming from directly beneath them.

Amanda nudged him in the ribs. "There it is!"

His eyes followed her outstretched hand and he saw what was making her so excited. An open olive green crate protruded from the shadows on the other side of the factory, partially obscured by one of the defunct machines. Inside the crate was a conical device, around a meter long. Wires trailed from the device to a laptop computer, which they couldn't see from their position.

"Okay. It looks like there's no one guarding the warhead. We can do this." He took a deep, quiet breath. According to his watch, they had less than forty-five minutes until the bomb lit up the factory and central Moscow like the Fourth of July, vaporizing their bodies into a billion glowing atoms.

"Let's spread out about twenty meters so we have multiple angles of fire. I want to see who's beneath us," Amanda suggested quietly.

Kurt didn't argue. He made his way to the right, down the catwalk. Amanda went left. She had less distance to cover, as she would turn a corner and have a line of sight under their entrance point in a few meters. As Kurt was getting into position, there was a loud commotion below.

"Who's there?" a voice shouted in rapid-fire Russian.

Before either could respond, all hell broke loose.

Forty-Six

THE FIRST SHOT CAME FROM somewhere across the room. Two inches to the left and it would have taken off Amanda's head. As it was, she felt the heat of the bullet as it whizzed by and ricocheted off the catwalk railing. She ducked, cursing herself for not paying better attention. She held her gun over the railing and fired off two quick shots in the shooter's general direction, and then scuttled to her left, seeking cover behind a rusty iron pipe.

Twenty feet away, she saw that Kurt was having his own issues. With the element of surprise gone, he was a sitting duck. The apparent rebel leader, a bearded man of indeterminate age, screamed and dashed toward the bomb. A bullet *spanged* off the other side of the pipe, and then everything went silent.

She ventured a glance around her cover, trying to check Kurt's position. He was no better off than she was. Crouched behind an identical pipe, he gave her a worried look and shook his head as if to say, "There's no way."

She wasn't ready to give up yet. She fired again.

Once. Twice. *Click. Click.* "Shit!" She was out of bullets. Ejecting the empty magazine with one hand, she grabbed another from her pocket and jammed it home, raked the slide to chamber a round.

As she was about to rain fire onto the factory floor again, Kurt yelled, "Amanda! Behind you!" She swung around, searching for the source of his alarm. The man who had disappeared at the beginning of the shootout, the man she had assumed was running to protect the bomb, had flanked her and was ascending a set of spiral stairs with his AK-47 at the ready.

She spun and put two shots into the man's face, sending him tumbling down the stairwell, his gun discharging in a wild burst as it crashed to the factory floor. *That's one*, she thought with bitter satisfaction. *How many more are there?*

The rebels, seeing their leader lose his life on the stairs, made no further attempts. They knew all they had to do was run out the clock. At the same time, she and Kurt were pinned down. The rebels had excellent cover and were able to defend their positions with little effort. She checked her watch. It was smashed, broken in the firefight. She had no idea how much time they had left.

Kurt's right, she thought. *There's no way. We're going to die here.* She felt sick at the thought of making it so far, getting so close. She could barely see the bomb from her position behind the pipe, but its presence was impossible to ignore. It meant instant death for her, Kurt, and everyone within ten miles or more.

The air was thick with the scent of cordite and old grease. she heard footsteps below, followed by frantic whispering. Then, through the ringing in her ears, she heard something else. She cupped her ear. *Is that...?* The distinctive whump-whump of a low-flying military helicopter, hovering above. *No*, she realized. *Not one. Several.*

One of the men below stepped from his hiding spot. She put two into his chest, dropping him where he stood. That triggered another furious round of gunfire as the men below retaliated for their fallen compatriot. Just as she thought she couldn't stand it anymore, there was a series of loud crashes on the roof over her head, boots, moving fast.

Turning, she saw four uniformed men burst through the door to her rear. The greasy skylight exploded, raining glass shards on the factory floor as another cluster of men fast-rappelled through empty space, guns blazing. Before she was shoved face-first to the floor, she saw a group of soldiers materialize behind Kurt and pile on top of him as well.

It was over in less than thirty seconds. Staccato bursts of gunfire rang out as the soldiers, Russian, Amanda realized, mopped up the Chechens on the factory floor.

"*Vse Yasno!* All clear!" she heard from several soldiers within the building. The man covering her extended a hand and helped her to her feet.

"How?" she asked, incredulous.

The soldier, a solid slab of killing muscle in his early twenties, shook his head as if to say he didn't speak English. He held up his left forearm, upon which were strapped pictures of both her and Kurt. He motioned for her to follow, tapping his wristwatch.

The bomb! She joined up with Kurt, and they raced

down the stairs to the warhead.

A small team of soldiers had clustered around the device; they were inspecting connections and tracing the wiring from the internals to the attached laptop computer.

"Who's in charge?" she asked in Russian, desperate for information.

"*I am the commander,*" a compact man with a close buzz-cut answered in English. He pointed away from the warhead. "Please stand over there."

She got the message loud and clear and took a step back.

A few seconds later, a young soldier barely out of his teens stepped away from the bomb and pulled the commander aside. They had a quick, hushed conversation in rapid-fire Russian, out of Amanda's earshot. The commander seemed to agree with whatever the soldier was saying.

With a quick smile, the soldier reached into the interior of the warhead and yanked with all of his might, straining as he did, until there was a loud pop. The smell of burnt electrical components permeated the air. The technician held up a fistful of wires and waved them in triumph.

The commander relaxed, his body sagging as the tension ran out of him like water down a drain. He turned and wobbled towards the building entrance where he leaned up against the wall for a moment before pitching forward and vomiting into a trash barrel.

She and Kurt raced to catch up to him, reaching him as he wiped the last traces of vomit from his lips. "Sir?" she started.

He held up his hand, motioning for them to wait. The color was creeping back into his face. He turned and strode through the door toward a slight man clad in Russian fatigues. He retrieved a mobile phone from the man and started speaking. After a moment of back and forth Russian, he offered the phone to Amanda.

She cocked her head, confused. "Who is it?"

Without answering, he pushed the phone into her outstretched hand.

"Hello?" she said into the phone.

"Hello, Ms. Carter. This is President Cooper."

The White House

AMANDA NUDGED KURT, AND WHISPERED, "Did you ever think you'd be here?"

He grinned, barely able to contain his excitement. It had been only two days since the Spetsnaz team had eliminated the rebels at the warehouse and defused the bomb, saving Moscow from nuclear annihilation. Those two days had been a whirlwind of debriefings by a host of civilian and military personnel, culminating in this final meeting with the president.

Still, he had no idea who employed Amanda. Every time he thought he was close to the answer, another piece of information emerged, sending him in a different direction. It frustrated him to no end. She was a testament to his brother, a living, breathing ball of contradictions. One thing was clear; they were inextricably joined by the events of the past days, fused in a new and strange partnership that neither of them quite understood.

Immediately after the incident in Moscow, they had been transported to Sheremetyevo Airport by the

Russian security services and placed on an idling U.S. government Gulfstream V. From there, they had endured an agonizing flight to Andrews Air Force Base, outside of the Capital. It had happened so fast, it felt as if he was watching a movie, as if the events were happening to someone else.

He gave Amanda's hand a squeeze. She returned the pressure, her fingers brushing against his wrist in a promise of things to come. His heart soared when he looked into her eyes, and she mouthed, "Later." It was all he could do not to take her into his arms, feel her body against his and tell her how he felt. *Not here.*

The President's secretary received a call, then stood and motioned to them. "He's ready for you."

His battered muscles screaming in protest, he got to his feet, He forced himself to relax.

"Smile, Kurt. This is the fun part," Amanda whispered. He had to admit he was enjoying the attention. He had never experienced anything like this before, and he knew it was unlikely he ever would again. His only regret was that Amelia and Heidi weren't present to share in the excitement.

The president's secretary opened the door and ushered them in to the Oval Office. President Cooper was alone. He put down his pen and beamed at them. "Kurt! Amanda! Welcome. I'm so glad you could join me today!"

As if you turned down an invitation from the President.

"Thank you for seeing us, sir," Amanda responded for the both of them. *She's done this before*, Kurt realized with a start. The president got up and walked around his desk, motioning them towards a set of uncomfortable-looking couches.

He regarded them for a minute before speaking. "I'd like to start off by personally thanking the two of you for your bravery in Moscow. Without your actions, the world would be a very different place today, a place I think no one was prepared to deal with."

Individually, they thanked him, assuring him it was what anyone in their position would have done.

"And Mr. Vetter, I would also like to commend your brother. Although he's no longer with us, he's a true hero."

Feeling tears well up, Kurt looked at the floor. Mike was supposed to have been the star of the family, the one who had everything in the world going for him. "Thank you again, sir," he said, raising his eyes to the president's. "I'm sure Mike would appreciate your recognition."

"With that in mind," the president continued, "I'd like to present you both, and your brother posthumously, with the Presidential Medal of Freedom. Very few of these have been awarded in the history of our nation, and only for the most extraordinary of actions."

He opened a folder from his desk and handed across three heavyweight pages, two to Kurt and one to Amanda. Each page was liberally embossed with gold stamps. The president's signature was at the bottom of each. Kurt was confused. He thought the president had said *Medals* of Freedom.

"Since your involvement in this matter technically did not happen, and since Ms. Carter is not a U.S. citizen, your medals, and these documents, will be stored in a secure facility. Your brother's medal will be presented to his widow."

"Thank you, sir," Kurt said, understanding.

"Sir?" Amanda asked.

"Yes, Ms. Carter?"

"I still have one question." President Cooper raised his eyebrows inquisitively.

"How did the Russians know where to go?"

Kurt had been wondering this same thing. Neither of them had spoken with anyone after the Russians had deposited them at the airport.

The president cracked a smile. "Let me just say that President Sokolov and I go back a long way. We had a little man-to-man talk, against the advice of my advisors I must note, and worked out a deal."

Amanda's eyes grew large. "You called him up, just like that?"

"I did."

Kurt was impressed, his impression of this man he had not voted for rising considerably. He chewed on this news for a second. "Actually, sir, I have one more question as well."

"Go ahead."

"What happened to the CIA elements that started this whole thing? The people my brother worked for?"

"I'm afraid I can't comment on that," the president replied, his smile faltering.

Kurt expected this but was still disappointed. "I understand."

"Now, about your future," the president started. Before he could finish his sentence, there was an urgent knocking on the door, and then it burst open.

A team of Secret Service agents poured into the room with their side arms at the ready.

"What is it now?" the president snapped.

"Sir, you need to come with us right away," the woman leading the group demanded.

"Can't you see I'm in a meeting?" he barked, his face turning beet red with anger.

"Sir, there's been an explosion in Norfolk. Nuclear."

The room fell into shocked silence for a moment as the occupants digested the news.

President Cooper responded first. "What do you mean '*nuclear*?' I need details."

The secret service agent shook her head and reached for his arm. "We don't have any at the moment sir. Our job is to get you to a safe location. We need to move right now!"

The president looked at Kurt and Amanda with dismay, like a man who has climbed a mountain only to discover the true summit is still far above. "They're coming with me," the president said, gesturing at them.

They looked at each other, and simultaneously whispered, "Another bomb?"

The lead agent considered the president's command for a heartbeat, and then sprang into action.

As a group, they dashed from the oval office onto the lawn of the White House, where Marine One was already waiting.

ABOUT THE AUTHOR

William Esmont lives in Southern Arizona with his wife, their three dogs, and one cat. *The Patriot Paradox* is his second novel, and the first in a series of espionage thrillers following the adventures of Kurt Vetter.